AN AMERICAN ROMANCE

Hans Koning

Allison & Busby
Published by W.H. Allen & Co. Plc

An Allison & Busby book
Published in 1989 by
W.H. Allen & Co. Plc
Sekforde House
175/9 St John St
London EC1V 4LL

First published in Great Britain by Faber & Faber in 1961

Printed in Great Britain by
Courier International Ltd, Tiptree, Essex

ISBN 0 7490 0025 2

1

WHEN I woke up in the shaking light of dawn, I saw her lying next to me, her head turned away and her short dark hair pushed upward from her neck by the pillow.

It was such a girlish neck, and I wanted to put out my hand and touch it. But then I discovered that my eyes were still closed, and that I was not awake. I struggled to open them, and the dawn was in the room, but she was not -- there was only the sheet, and a corner of the striped box spring sticking out. There was no one there but me.

2

WHEN the bus pulled into the New York City terminal, he had seventeen cents left. It had been a long ride from Los Angeles.

Amarillo in Texas, two days earlier, had been his last night in bed, and when he walked from the tourist home to the bus station there in the bright freezing sunlight and counted his money it was less than three dollars, to last to New York.

Yet it hadn't been hard; only the last night from Raleigh north when the driver no longer put out the light and the people remained standing and talking in the aisle between stops, did it become like a ride through an endless city.

He was glad that his money had run out. Lack of money at least gave sense to a cross-country bus trip – the half-nauseous shaking along for all those miles, with the only colour the colour in the names of the towns called out by the driver in front of identical bus stations.

He came out on the sidewalk and caught a glimpse of himself in a strip of mirror bordering a shop window – a tall, rather thin young man looking a bit shabby in his raincoat on a cold winter morning. He started walking towards Fifth Avenue with his suitcase. I am entering New York, he thought, without name or money, ready to be swallowed up by it, vanish in its darkest heart, be a tramp. Something exciting and at the same time sheltering. Or play D'Artagnan riding into Paris. New York is the city now, the way Paris was once.

He decided to telephone an old friend of his, a man called John Gregg. Gregg listened to his story and then told him to come over to his office in a taxi.

'I'll come down and pay your fare,' Gregg said. 'And Philip...'

'Yes?'

'Did you shave today?' Gregg asked.

'Oh yes, electrically, on the outlet of a New Jersey jukebox.'

'In that case, I'll take you to lunch,' Gregg answered.

3

THE Greggs gave a party when Philip had been staying with them for some days. There were two businessmen with their wives, an engineer who had brought along a pretty girl from Boston, a couple teaching at Columbia, and a South American girl who was an interpreter at the United Nations.

Philip had been wandering all over town that day, and he felt tired and bored. He wasn't making any impression on the others either, he thought.

Dorothy Gregg asked him to tell about Los Angeles and his work there. Several faces turned towards him, but Philip didn't make much of the occasion. 'Oh, just some messing around for a television station, NBC News,' he said. He wanted to say more, but attention drifted away from him again.

The following day he called the South American girl and invited her to dinner. She said yes, and he borrowed ten dollars from John Gregg, to be repaid as soon as he had a job.

Ten dollars wasn't much for dining out, and Philip took the girl to a rather shabby Italian restaurant and ordered wine instead of cocktails.

'I know this is like one of the movies,' he said. 'They're always having girls on dates in New York taken to little Italian restaurants with checked table-cloths. But I picked this place only because I'm slightly broke, temporarily. Definitely not for local colour.'

The girl looked at him with serious eyes and said, 'I like Italian food.'

Philip had told himself to be very psychological, not to rush things, bide his time and just shake hands when saying goodbye. But over the coffee the girl started telling him about the various men she met in New York, how they always made passes at her on the first evening out and how if she refused they never called again. It all sounded slightly incongruous; she had such a solemn voice.

Philip had to swallow at that 'if' in 'if I refuse', he laughed and said, 'They should be more clever – it's not the thing to show you're in such a hurry.'

The girl answered, 'Well, you know, I always decide right away whether I want to make love to a man or not.'

Philip thought that the only answer to that could be 'Would you want to with me?'

The girl looked at him, from him to the empty wine bottle, and then she said firmly, 'No.'

'Oh,' Philip answered.

After that exchange he took her home on the bus. He never saw her again.

4

THE following morning Philip went to see a non-committal man at NBC about a job, and after that he walked up Fifth Avenue.

It was a grey morning and a cold and dirty February wind was blowing in from across the Park.

A girl passed him, then stood still and said, 'Hello, how are you?' She was wearing a raincoat with the collar turned up and a kerchief over her head. It took him a moment to recognize her; she was the girl from Boston who had been at the party. She saw his hesitation and blushed.

'I'm Ann Sevier,' she said. 'We met at the Greggs'.'

'Of course. You're sort of hidden today.'

'That's my luck. When I put up my hair in pins I always run into someone I know.'

Philip laughed. They looked at each other for a moment. How different she is today, he thought. A woman has so many faces.

'When are you going back?' he finally asked.

She pointed at the large old house on the corner. 'I'm staying in New York. I got a job there. It's an educational foundation.'

'That's fast work,' Philip said wishfully.

'I was with a project of theirs in Cambridge.'

Dust swirled around them on a gust of wind. She shivered.

'I guess I shouldn't keep you standing on street corners on a day like this,' Philip said. 'Good luck with your job. Hope I'll be seeing you.'

'Good-bye,' she answered.

5

ON Thursday, two days later, the NBC man called Philip and said there might be some work for him in Public Service programmes. 'We're going to do a weekly half-hour on education,' he told him. 'Could you bring me some texts on high-school reform, four-hundred-word pieces?'

'Oh yes,' Philip answered, trying to sound enthusiastic. 'When do you want them?'

'A week from now is soon enough. And we'll pay you whether we use them or not.'

'I don't know a thing about high schools or why they should be reformed,' Philip told John Gregg, 'but I realize I have to earn some money soon.'

'Why don't you ask Ann Sevier to help you?' Gregg said. 'She works in education.'

'I know. How did you know?'

'But we're old friends – that's why she was here last week.'

'I thought it was just that that engineer had brought her along.'

'I had lunch with her yesterday and she asked about you. So there you are. You're too lazy, Philip, isn't that the real story? Never mind, we'll keep you a little longer. You're sure you don't want to teach? I could help you there.'

'I'm sure. I hate it.'

'And why did you study philosophy then?' Gregg asked.

'Oh, to be taught, I guess. Only I wasn't.'

When Philip called Ann Sevier she said she would be happy to get together whatever material she could find on the subject.

On Friday afternoon he went over to her office. His name was telephoned up and he stood in the lobby watching the visitors. They were mainly students; they have such sophisticated faces, he thought. New York is quite a city.

Then he saw Ann. She looks even prettier than that night

at the party, he said to himself, I hope the engineer realizes what he's got. She gave him the file she had made and explained it to him. 'Call me if you have any problems with it,' she said.

'I really don't know how to thank you,' Philip answered. 'It must have seemed a terrible imposition, asking you this.'

'Not at all. That's part of the work we're supposed to do. We're being noble and non-profit all day long here.'

6

PHILIP called her Saturday morning, for on re-reading what he had written the night before he thought that it was awful. 'Why don't you ask her over?' John Gregg shouted from the other room, and then came to the telephone himself and asked Ann to come for lunch. She said she would.

The four of them ate in the large living-room on the ground floor of the Greggs' house. She is such a sunny girl, Philip thought. And knowing that she was the engineer's girl friend – he had asked Gregg about that – he felt pleased simply looking at her and talking with her. She was not just being helpful; strange as it seemed to him, she enjoyed the idea of working on his high-school texts.

She came upstairs with him when lunch was over; she knelt on a chair at the window of his room and looked out over the East River glittering in the sunlight. What lovely ankles she has, he discovered. Dorothy Gregg brought them their coffee, Ann read his text and they decided it wasn't so bad after all. 'Don't bother with that file any more,' she said. 'If you bring John's typewriter here I can dictate you an outline for the rest.'

'I'm very ashamed to let you do all the work,' Philip said while typing, 'but don't think I don't love it. If I get the programme I'll cut you in.'

'You mean you're going to make me a star?' Ann asked with fluttering eyelashes.

He began to laugh.

'You don't really want this job, do you?' she said.

'No, I guess not. But I've stayed with John for more than a week already, and I must get a place of my own and pay my debts. Then I'll start looking for something more solid.'

'Why did you come to New York?' she asked.

'It's hard to explain. I like California, and I like the Southland – that's what they call the Los Angeles part of it, sort of – it's different from any other place in America. But it's vacuous, you know. I needed a look at life.'

Why did I come here? he thought. It was an attack of sharp restlessness which had got him on the bus east; a feeling like nostalgia, but nostalgia for a place not yet found, a feeling which made him want to look for something or someone so new and unseen that he could not even know what he was searching for.

'Where are you from?' she asked.

'I was born in Portland, in Oregon, but I grew up in California. My parents are dead.'

She stood up. 'I did enjoy our session,' she said. 'I have to go now. Let me know how you make out.'

'I will,' he answered. 'And you know how grateful I am for your help.'

She said good-bye to the Greggs and he walked her to the door. He waited until she had vanished around the corner and then he came out into the street too. He walked over to the parapet and looked down at the river; he leaned on the cold wall with his hands, pushed himself up and sat down on it.

He kicked with his heels against the stone and he suddenly thought that he was very happy with life and with himself.

7

THE following day, Sunday, Philip found himself taking a subway to the Battery and wandering through the empty streets; he went to the point of the land and sat on a bench against the wall of what looked like an imitation fortress. I must make inventory of my life and my future, he thought; but as he sat there, staring at the false sheen of the sun on the ruffled water, his only awareness was his being there, in the weak February sunlight, on the hard sharp wood of the bench.

He went to look for a cafeteria to eat lunch but everything was closed, and then, seeing a cigar store open, he went in and telephoned Ann.

She didn't sound surprised at all.

'If you want to come over later,' she said, 'I'll make you tea and play you some records.'

Philip didn't want to go back to the Greggs' house so he walked around and sat on benches until it was three; then he took a bus to her apartment which was in the East Seventies.

She is blushing, he thought when she opened the door, no, it must be the light. 'Hello,' he said to her, 'I'm frozen. What a foul climate this city has. God knows why we're living here. What a nice place you have.'

He was surprised: a very sleek modern room, with a red couch, a low marble table, many books, and a warm light inverting the bleakness of the city outside.

She smiled at him.

'You must have done all this so fast,' he said.

'They're all my things from Boston – I took this place because I could see they'd fit here more or less. Now I'll make that tea I promised you. You do look cold.'

She went to the kitchen and he got up again, had a glimpse of himself in a mirror and rubbed his white face, then stood around and looked at the titles on her bookshelves.

'A lot of my books are still at home,' she said, coming back into the room. 'You can have a drink too, you know.'

'Tea is fine,' Philip said. 'What did you study in college?'

'English lit.,' she said, 'Radcliffe, class of fifty-six.'

She saw on his face that he was computing her age from that and laughed. 'How old are you?' she asked.

'Twenty-six. How nice it is here, Ann.'

She did not answer, she seemed not to have listened. 'Do you want to hear some French songs?' she then said.

She played records, and they talked.

It was a quiet afternoon, but it had a quality of happiness, he thought; there was no need to explain why he had telephoned – it was all very natural. He knew that he should leave soon because she was bound to have a date with her engineer and she'd want to change first – she was wearing a nondescript dress, rather dowdy actually, he thought; she is tall and she has a pretty figure but it isn't obvious – except for her long legs. She can't hide those. She is understating her body. 'Do you believe in understatement?' he asked her.

'Yes, I guess so. Not about things that really matter. I like people who get excited or furious at times.'

Philip grinned. 'I'd get excited about it,' he said.

'About what?'

'Nothing. I was having a joke with myself. I must go now. Thank you for having me here.'

'Thank you for coming.'

As he was getting up, he picked up a little red scarf which was lying next to him on the couch. He sat down again, for a moment, and without knowing why, in a kind of playfulness, he bent over and bound it around her ankle. She looked at him, smiled fleetingly but did not comment, and she left it there when she got up to let him out.

13

8

ON Monday Philip was called by a man he knew in the New York office of the State Department. It was about an Asian news agency which was supposed to be looking for an American to edit their bulletins. Philip went there, and an hour later he found himself with a job. It was a far from exciting one: preparing a daily news sheet from a series of teletype messages which were about stock-market prices, shipping, and plantations. But it was a job; it paid eighty dollars a week, and he decided he was not going to let it pass while waiting for the NBC people to make up their minds.

He called John Gregg.

'I took a job, just now. Starting next Monday.'

'Well, congratulations,' Gregg said.

'I'll go and find a place to live. And I owe you forty-seven dollars and fifty cents.'

Gregg laughed. 'There's no hurry,' he said, 'I trust you, up to fifty dollars. Come over for lunch and tell me about your new career.'

'All right, I will. And I'm buying it.'

'You?' Gregg asked. 'Are you on an expense account already?'

Out in the street, Philip thought that there was something nice and secure about working in Rockefeller Centre – the news agency was in the Associated Press Building. It's the quintessence of belonging, he said to himself – but the thrill of that will probably wear off quickly enough.

He went to NBC and handed in his high-school script. The secretary had a cheque of fifty dollars for him all made out. 'We're not always that prompt,' she told him. 'This must be my day,' Philip said, surprised.

He lunched with Gregg and walked him back to his office, and as he was left standing alone on the sidewalk, he thought, I feel in control of things, I'm landing on my feet. He was so pleased with the idea that he decided to go see Ann; he couldn't keep it to himself.

He went to the Foundation and straight up to her floor. As he came out of the elevator he caught sight of her talking to another girl. She saw him at the same moment, and she blushed deeply – this time he was certain of it. It confused him, he couldn't think what it meant.

He went over to her. 'Forgive me for bursting in here like this,' he said.

'But I'm glad to see you,' Ann answered, walking away from the other girl with a nod. 'How are things?'

'I have a job – but I must tell you about that another time. I also got paid for the high schools. I wanted to ask you if you'd have a drink with me on the strength of that.'

'I'd love to – but you don't have to do it, you know.'

'But I want to.'

'All right, then,' she said. 'Tomorrow?'

'May I come here and pick you up?'

'Yes, I'll be through at half past five.'

'See you tomorrow at half past five,' Philip said. She walked him to the elevator, he shook hands with her formally, solemnly almost; they looked at each other as the elevator doors closed between them.

9

IT was dark when Philip came to Ann's building and it was freezing hard. He was early; he told the receptionist he had come to get someone and would just wait in the lobby. He walked over to a huge mirror hanging over a mantelpiece oddly bisected by a partition. God, I look shabby, he thought, I must buy some clothes if I'm going to stay in New York. I will stay.

The idea of settling there, which until then he had never considered, now of a sudden seemed obvious. Perhaps it's because I'm getting too old for this wandering around, he told himself. He combed his hair, took off his raincoat and put it over his arm. It looked better that way.

He sat down on the arm of an easy chair in a corner. It was only quarter past five. He wasn't really capable of formulating why he was there, why he had invited Ann Sevier for a drink. It had all become part of the same drive which had made him leave his news job in Los Angeles, a girl friend, and a house in the Hollywood Hills.

It was a shock suddenly to see Ann come down the wide marble staircase. He had been watching the people bursting out of the little elevator, but something made him look around, and her appearance impressed itself upon him with a strange clarity. He saw her from her feet up: first her elegant high-heeled shoes, her long legs, a white wool dress, her wide mouth, her short dark hair. She was carrying a black fur coat over her arm and held a pocket-book by its straps.

He went over to her and she held out her hand as a greeting. They put their coats on and then they were out in the street, brushed by hasty passers-by; and without speaking much they walked up Madison Avenue against a dark and biting wind, to the bar of a hotel in the Sixties.

There was no one there when they came in. They sat in a corner and she asked for a Martini. Neither of them said a word until their drinks had been brought and they had drunk them down as if they were in a great hurry. Then they looked at each other and laughed.

Philip began to feel utterly light-headed and reckless. He started telling her about his new job, but without listening to his own words and with the feeling that it didn't matter what he said, that there was some sudden understanding between them and their conversation just a front, like secret agents exchanging information in the guise of a chat. She told him about the Foundation and about her parents' house in Boston. 'It's really Brookline. But when you say that here people think you mean Brooklyn.'

'I've been there,' he said, 'very quiet and green and towny. Let's have another drink.'

'Will you be happy doing a news bulletin?' she asked.

'It's strictly pot-boiling.'

'What do you want of life?'

'What do you want?'

'I asked first,' she said.

He looked at her and then at the waiter, an old man, who was leaning in a corner against the bar and who averted his eyes.

'I don't really know,' he said. 'After the Army and college I started with teaching; I had done philosophy at Berkeley. Then I immediately stopped again. That was four years ago. I do want to do real work, important things; I will one day, I hope. But I'm not interested in work right now; work is just something I have to do. I know that sounds awful. I can't stay put, I feel on a kind of search –'

'Don't tell me you're that young,' Ann said plaintively, 'don't say that you want to be a bum and on the road.'

'Oh God no, I'm not escaping from myself, it has to do with love, with a woman.'

'A real one?'

'A dreamt one.'

'Now you sound like a knight.'

'Oh, I like that better than sounding like a bum.'

There was a silence.

'Did you ever think what psychiatry would have done to knighthood?' she said. 'Ruined it, nipped it in the bud, but definitely. "When did you first feel this urge to go to Jerusalem?"'

He looked at her. She smiled.

'Why do you smile?' asked Philip.

'I just felt like smiling at you,' she said.

'Do you believe in – ?' he began.

'No,' she said hastily.

'Ann, are you free? Are you a free woman?' he asked.

'Free? Yes, I am. Free and lost. Or I was.'

'Was?'

'I always felt free and lost – not in a miserable way – happily lost.'

'And now?'

She didn't answer.

'Could we have one more drink?' she asked. 'My God, it's late. I have a class on Tuesday nights.'

'At what time?'

'Eight. But I should eat something first, I guess,' she said, her voice trailing off.

'Well, a quick one, and then I'll walk you over to the subway or wherever you're going.'

She went out into the street, he followed her, stumbling through the revolving door, but he wasn't drunk. 'I'm dizzy,' he said to her.

They stood on the deserted sidewalk.

'It's cold,' Ann murmured.

'Yes.' He took a hesitant step, and stopped. He put his hands against her cheeks and kissed her on her eyes and then on her mouth.

'I'm sorry,' he whispered.

They walked a few feet and when he stopped again, she did too. She held her face up; he looked at her mouth from very close. They shivered when they kissed.

'The first time I saw you I thought, What a beautiful face that man has,' Ann said.

He looked shy. 'You did? Then why didn't you talk to me that evening?'

'But I tried to. You didn't pay the least attention to me. In fact, you didn't recognize me the next day.'

'You were the only pretty woman at that party. The only woman. But you weren't alone.'

He leaned against the door of a shop, sheltered against the wind, he put his arms around her and pressed her against him.

He lifted her up, swung her around and put her down again. He swayed for a moment.

'It's just the gin,' she announced. 'Euphoria. Tomorrow we'll feel awful.'

'Euphoria,' Philip repeated with disgust. 'You blue-stocking, I love you, I love your short hair and your long legs. Do you love me?'

She laughed happily and did not answer.

'Look at that hard sky,' he cried. 'It must be freezing hun-

18

dreds of degrees. I should get you something to eat. Let's run and get warm.'

He took her hand and pulled her with him. 'What about your class?' he asked.

'I've missed it. I don't care.'

She stood still. 'Kiss me,' she said.

'I'm so sorry I have no place of my own yet,' Philip said. 'Ann, can't we go to yours?'

'No, we can't,' she answered.

'I . . . I didn't mean . . .'

She looked at him. 'I'd like to,' she said. 'I want to. But John is sitting there, waiting for me to get home.'

'John? John Gregg?'

'John Irwin. You met him.'

'The engineer? Is he your boy friend?'

'Yes, he is. We're getting married.'

He stopped again, put his hands on her shoulders, and stared into her face. And then he felt so exuberant that he thought, I can do anything, I'm capable of anything.

'Are you?' he asked, laughing at her.

She held her head sideways, and she said, 'No, Philip, perhaps I'm not.'

10

THEY wandered for a long time through the empty streets. He felt in a daze, they talked haphazardly, and they kissed and held each other in shop entrances and at corners until they heard steps approaching and then they walked on again.

She stood still in front of a darkened store window, and said in an unexpectedly firm voice, 'Now I'm very cold. And I must get home.'

'Yes,' he said. 'I'll find us a cab.'

When they were sitting in their taxi he asked, 'Will he still be there?'

19

'Perhaps. He must be furious. I should have phoned – what a terrible way to behave,' Ann said.

'Will you tell him, about us?'

'Yes, of course,' Ann said.

'Tonight?'

'No, not tonight. I must think first about what to say – I don't want to make him miserable. It's a nasty thing to do.'

'Yes,' Philip said tonelessly.

'And then you'll go back to Los Angeles and there I'll be, living and dying an old maid,' Ann said.

They looked at each other and then they looked away. Suddenly they were both shy. How did I ever find the courage, he thought, she is such a complete human being, she is so grown-up, how can a man intrude upon that?

'Ann?' he asked.

'Yes?'

'If I had asked you to come to a hotel with me tonight, would you have?'

'Yes, of course I would,' she answered. 'And I'm almost angry with you for not asking.'

He covered his face with his hands in half-pretended embarrassment.

'Philip, would you mind getting off at the corner?' she asked. 'You know, just in case. I do want to handle things carefully.'

He kissed her hand and got out, and without looking back he almost ran down the avenue and to the Greggs' house.

At the Greggs' the lights were all out, but Philip went up to their bedroom and knocked.

'What is it?' he heard Dorothy's surprised voice after a moment.

'It's me, Philip. May I come in?'

'Er ... yes, certainly. But don't put the light on,' Dorothy said when he entered. 'Just leave the door open.'

Philip sat down on the rug beside their bed and laughed. 'Sorry to wake you,' he said. 'I just had to.'

'Is he drunk?' John asked without raising his head from the pillow. 'And what time is it?'

'One,' Dorothy answered. 'I guess he is.'

20

'No, I'm not,' Philip said. 'I'm in love.'

'Well, that's splendid news. And who's the fortunate girl?'

'Ann – Ann Sevier.'

'What!' John cried, suddenly lifting his head. 'Ann? Did you go out with her this evening?'

'Yes,' Philip said.

'Is she in love with you too?'

'Yes.'

'Did she say so?'

'Yes.'

John and Dorothy looked at each other and then at Philip.

'And what about that man she was going to marry next month?' John asked in an amused voice.

'Next month? Jesus. Well, she isn't going to, I guess,' Philip said.

'Good heavens,' Dorothy said. 'I hope you won't make her regret that.'

'Hadn't you better go to bed?' John asked.

Philip stood up and kissed Dorothy on the cheek. 'Good night,' he said.

'Congratulations!' they both cried as he closed the door behind him.

11

PHILIP called Ann at precisely half past nine in the morning and the girl who picked up her telephone said, 'Just a moment, Ann is walking in right now.'

'Yes?' Ann said, 'Hello? Who is it?'

'It's me – Philip. I was standing here just breathing. I didn't dare speak the first words. I wondered so how you'd sound.'

She laughed. 'Good morning Phil.'

'Oh, don't call me Phil. Or do. Call me anything. As long as you go on calling.'

Then he added, 'Ann, will I see you tonight?'

She answered. 'Could you come over at lunch-time? I want to talk to you about tonight.'

He swallowed. 'Is anything wrong?'

'Nothing at all.' And she added in an assuring whisper, 'I love you.'

He went over to the Foundation at noon and they walked to a coffee shop. He had been unable to do anything in the morning but pace up and down in his room; he had had the greatest trouble stopping himself from calling her again or going over there too early.

'Oh, Ann, how fresh and lovely and sunny you look!' he said to her. 'Whom are you going out with tonight?'

He had thought that she would laugh, but she said, 'With John Irwin. He has theatre tickets for tonight, we're going with two other people.'

'Oh.'

'Please don't be sour about it. He's had them for months, I didn't have the heart to say no now. I'm going straight home afterward, alone.'

'I understand.'

'I will tell him about us. I couldn't quite muster the courage last night. But I will this week, I promise you. Or have you changed your mind?'

'No, Annie, I haven't changed my mind,' he said. 'Can you sit here alone for a few minutes? I have something urgent to do.'

He left the coffee shop and ran over to the hotel where they had had their drink the evening before.

He slowly crossed the lobby.

'I want a room, for one night,' he told the clerk. 'Mr and Mrs Andersen. We just arrived.'

'Sign here, sir,' the clerk said.

'I'm leaving everything except a bag at La Guardia,' Philip said, 'so perhaps I'd better pay now.'

'As you wish,' the clerk replied. 'When will you want your room?'

'Right now, as soon as we're through with lunch, we're tired. We want to rest a bit before going out. And could you have some coffee sent up?'

22

He went back to the coffee shop as fast as he could.

'Ann,' he asked, 'will you come with me?'

He walked her to the hotel and they stopped in front of the entrance. 'I have a room here,' he said.

She blushed and looked hard at him.

'Please come,' he said.

She was thinking. 'Please go in and wait for me in the lobby,' she answered.

He sat down in a leather armchair and closed his eyes. His heart was pounding.

She came in a few minutes later and stood still by his chair.

'All I did was go around the block once,' she said. 'You know, it's a big decision.'

He got up. She smiled at him and walked ahead of him to the huge cast-iron gate of the elevator.

12

IT was a nice room, a studio with daybeds under dark-red covers. They sat at the table near the window, and a girl knocked and carried in a coffee tray. In silence Ann poured their coffee, he took a sip from his cup and put it down again. She got up and sat on one of the couches.

He went over to her and kissed her on her hair.

'Please take off your dress,' he said almost inaudibly.

She undressed with her back turned towards him and then lay down, her eyes closed. He lay next to her and held her in his arms, and said, 'You have the most beautiful back, Ann.'

He did not caress her, he came into her and whispered, 'Is it safe?'

She nodded, and suddenly they were very wild and quick.

Only then did she open her eyes and look at him. 'Hello,' he said.

'I don't know why you make me so shy,' she murmured.

'You me.'

What a beautiful girl she is, he thought, amazed almost. She is so elegant, and firm, warm, her soft skin – my God. 'But you're a perfect beauty,' he said to her.

'I know I have good legs,' she told him, smiling.

'You have good everything. I get dizzy just looking at you.'

She turned towards him and followed the line of his body with her hand. 'You're nice too,' she said, 'and you're so tall.'

When he came back into her they lay still like that for a long time; he felt enveloped, drowning in her warmth, one long overwhelming caress which turned all his thoughts to one point. And after he had had her, he went on feeling that way with hardly any break, 'Oh I am am am in love with you,' he said.

They did drink their coffee, cold.

They marched through the lobby and out of the hotel talking hard and without looking at anybody.

'It's quarter to four,' she said horrified when they had come to her office.

'Oh, hell – is that fatal?'

'No,' she said in a very soft voice; she looked at him and closed her eyes for a moment as a good-bye, then she turned and vanished into the building.

13

PHILIP did not get to see her again until Friday, two days later. He had a cheerless time, wandering along the East Side and through the Village with the *Times* apartment ads, sitting in double-feature movie houses on Forty-second Street – he had no peace to do anything real and he built his hours around the long telephone conversations he had with her. At NBC he was told that he might be asked for free-lance contributions to the programme.

So his last free days went by. 'It's a Japanese custom,' Gregg said to him. 'In Japan after one day the bride goes back to her parents for a while. It's very sound psychology.'

Philip didn't stop thinking about Ann. He told himself, with amazement almost, that here he had suddenly met a woman who was about perfect, who had the most beautiful body he had ever seen, who had a sharp mind, who was uncynical and warm, and who had yet through some mystery fallen in love with him. And why hadn't she married before, or why, any-way, was she not pursued by glamorous and rich boy friends with whom he would never have been able to compete? Why had she planned to marry that rather pedestrian engineer?

It seemed too good to be true and he felt more and more in a hurry to consolidate his conquest before it would be undone by some stroke of fate; he also had a tremendous desire to talk about it, for people to know about it. She had asked him to wait with that which added to his state of agitation.

On Friday at lunch-time she met him in the cafeteria in the Park. He jumped up when he saw her coming and felt over-whelmingly relieved and happy. They walked together under a cold thin sun; he took her hand, she smiled at him, and only then did they start talking. '

'I've had a terrible time,' he said. 'Here I am a knight in Jerusalem, told to go wait at the gate a bit.'

'Don't be in such a hurry,' she said, laughing.

'But I am. I'm in a panic that you'll change your mind. And I'm jealous.'

She looked perturbed and he was sorry for his words.

'Did you tell him?' he asked.

'Yes, last night.'

'Was it bad?'

'Yes. And he cried.'

'Oh God,' Philip said.

'Let's not talk about it. I don't want to think about it now. It's over and done.' And she went on, 'I have to go to Brook-line tonight, Philip, for the week-end, to my parents.'

'Oh no!' Philip cried.

She stood still and pulled his head towards her, and kissed him. 'Don't think I'm casual,' she said. 'I was getting into some-

25

thing I didn't really want, and I'm so very relieved. I have an enormous urge now to straighten things out immediately. I have to tell my parents, in person.'

'Why?'

'They are preparing my wedding with John, Philip,' she said.

'I see. I'm sorry, Annie.'

'I like that name – Annie.'

'That's a poem by Poe. "And the fever called Living is conquered at last."'

'I know. "For Annie." I knew it by heart when I was in high school. I don't think I quite realized what it was all about, though.'

'I'm not sure I do now,' he said. 'But I like his naphthaline river of passion.'

'Did you know that poem before you met me?' she asked.

'No, I read it last night, in the Public Library. I sat there till it closed. Next to a very sad old man sleeping over the World Almanac. The Greggs are wonderful, but I'm not fit to live there any more and chat and watch TV. I go crazy. But all the places I've looked at are so crummy.'

'Will you take me to the station at six?'

'Yes, of course,' he said.

In the bus to the station – Ann refused a taxi – she gave him a key.

'Here's the key to my apartment,' she told him, 'I want you to stay there over the week-end. That way you'll have privacy and books and things – and no conversations to keep up with Dorothy.'

'Oh, Ann, how sweet of you,' he said. 'Are you sure?'

'Yes of course.'

'Suppose I start reading your letters?'

'You can read everything,' Ann said and added with a smile, 'but I hope you won't.'

'And if he calls.'

'He won't.'

He put her on the train and kissed her, and waved until the train itself had vanished from sight. Then he went to her apartment. At the corner of Third Avenue he first bought some cans of food and fruit for the week-end.

When he opened her door his heart was beating in his throat. He put his groceries down, then he found the light switch. He closed and locked the door behind him, and fell into a chair with his coat still on. He stretched his legs in front of him and felt inordinately happy.

14

AFTER a while Philip got up, took his bag to the kitchen and opened a can of soup. He decided to eat it out of the pot, and he walked through the living-room with his pan and spoon while he studied each object, book, magazine, photograph.

Then he put his things in the sink and opened the bedroom door. Ann had a wide bed, with a night table and a lamp on each side. There was a long dresser of whitish wood with a mirror over it all along its length, and a wall closet. He opened it and looked at her dresses and the neat row of her shoes. He opened a drawer and pulled out some of her underwear and felt it; this is a terrible thing to do, he thought, but he was grinning at himself at the same time. What pretty things she has, he thought, what lovely creatures women are. He let himself fall back on her bed and stared at the ceiling. Then his eye caught a portrait of the engineer standing on the dresser. He jumped up to study it, then turned it towards the wall. Finally he put it back the way it had been.

Philip was now suddenly struck by the idea that that man must have been in the room often, and that he and Ann had slept in the bed. It didn't make him jealous, but it perturbed him in an odd way; he felt as if he should exorcise the ghosts of ideas and emotions lived through there. He opened the window as wide as possible and let the icy wind hit into the room. Then he took two blankets with him for sleeping on the couch in the living-room, turned off the light and closed the door behind him.

He was lying on the couch, the room was dimly lit by a street lamp, when the telephone rang. It was Ann.

'How's my tenant?' she asked.

'Hello Ann! I'm so longing for you,' Philip said. 'I didn't want to answer the phone first but then I decided I could. Did you get to Boston all right?'

'Yes, and the train was even on time.'

'I bet you were accosted by that greying man who sat opposite you,' Philip said.

She laughed. 'He did ask me how long I was going away for, and when I answered "for the week-end", he said you had been waving as if it was for ever.'

'But it seems for ever. And don't talk to strangers on trains. Didn't your mother tell you?'

'What are you doing?' she asked.

'I am lying on your couch and dreaming of your beautiful breasts.'

She didn't answer for a moment. He asked, 'Shouldn't I have said that?'

'Oh yes, you should,' she said. And then: 'I'll be back on Sunday. It's all working out. My parents are very sweet about it. Please be a good boy.'

A singular thought: her trusting him so much that she was completely reorganizing her life; he played for a moment with the idea of the scoundrel he might have been, the note on the table, 'Dear Ann, I'm sorry but – ', It was a fearful fantasy. Then he let the truth re-enter him – that she was right, that he would be her faithful servant; and there was a peacefulness in that such as he had never known.

15

PHILIP felt as if Ann's apartment was a bridgehead to hold, and he never left the house during the following two days.

Living in her place amidst her possessions gave him an intense sense of intimacy with her; it seemed unbelievable that he had hardly known her a week earlier.

Sunday afternoon, dusk falling, he was sitting at the window staring out, when the doorbell rang. He jumped.

It was Ann with her face glowing from the wind and her brown eyes so bright that they were almost grey. He kissed her cold mouth, and she said, 'Oh, I like finding you here!' and kissed him back. 'Philip,' she asked, 'would you go down and bring up a box I brought? I couldn't manage it.'

'Yes,' he said. 'Oh, am I glad to see you!'

When he came back into the room she had taken off her fur coat.

'How do you like my dress?' she said. 'My parents bought it for me yesterday.'

He sat down on the box and stared at her in her black dress.

'Oh Ann,' he said.

She laughed and made a turn. 'Do you like it? It's very simple. A bit tight. Not the fashion at all.'

'It's most incredibly exciting,' he answered. He stood up and embraced her. 'You overwhelm me,' he whispered. And taking her hand, 'Please come with me.'

'But I want to tell you about the week-end,' she protested as she followed him. She lay down on her bed and began to laugh again. 'I'm in a devilish mood,' she said. 'You may undress me.'

They made love very simply; he felt that she was trying to hold out as long as possible, and when she had to give in he did too.

The first thing she said afterwards was: 'Where did you learn to make love so beautifully?'

'Do I?'

'Don't get coy,' she said. 'You know you do. You must have had hundreds of girls.'

'I'm very innocent,' he said. 'I'm scared of you, Ann. I'm scared of your beauty.'

'That's a sweet compliment,' she said. And then, 'My body is yours, for you are the first man to make me aware of it.'

He didn't answer. He lay beside her and stared at the ceiling.

He took a deep breath. I like living in my body, he thought, there's a colour to things, everything is brighter. That is because of her.

'What's in the box?' he asked.

'Things I brought from home, books mainly. Do you want to see them?'

He dragged the box into the bedroom and she cut the string with her nail scissors. 'I brought my college books,' she said, 'and even things like this.' She held up a copy of *The Wizard of Oz*. 'I like them around me.'

'Ann,' he said, opening the book, 'what a wonderful ex-libris.'

She looked at his face. 'Dear, what is the matter?'

'I don't know. It's so saddening.'

'This book belongs to Ann Sevier', it said on the ex-libris.

Over those words was a woodcut, two children standing under a tree and looking longingly out over a bay. On it, at a distance, a ship was setting sail.

16

'MAY I stay?' he asked in the dark.

'Yes of course,' she said, falling asleep with her head on his shoulder.

He carefully rested his hand against her back. We did make love beautifully, he thought. It's possible to be very excited and very controlled at the same time. Emptied of all desire but without any reaction against that desire, he let his mind wander over the idea of making love, making love to Ann Sevier, being allowed to touch her, to reach the final intimacy with her, lie on her lovely body. Where had he read once that synchronization isn't the ultimate wisdom in love-making? But this was not like that, they weren't being clever; they almost couldn't help being completely together in it. It was like riding the same wave, no, that was a terrible image. Falling into the same blue sea together.

He touched her back with his lips. 'Oh, you're such a girl,' he whispered, 'I'm in love with you, like a high-school boy.' He extricated his arm very slowly from under her head and turned over.

He woke up from an alarm clock ringing and blinked at the day. Ann jumped out of bed and turned the clock off and came back into the room in a short black Chinese dressing gown.

He tried to smile at her. 'Good morning, Ann,' he said, rubbing his face.

'You need a shave,' she told him.

'And a haircut.'

'No, don't. I like your long hair,' she said, standing at the edge of the bed.

He kissed her hand and lay still with his eyes closed.

'What time do you have be at your news agency?' she asked.

'Ten, they said. May I walk you to your office?'

'Oh, yes. If you get up now we can have coffee together somewhere. I'm all out of it.'

He sat at the counter of the coffee shop with her and studied his reflection in the mirror. 'God,' he sighed, 'I look awful, are you sure I'm your lover?'

'Don't be so vain,' she said, catching his eye in the mirror. 'Why don't you look a bit at me instead?'

'You look too fresh and bright, it's absolutely demoralizing.'

'You are pale,' she admitted.

'I wish you had seen me in California.'

'I'm sure you look splendid with a tan,' she said.

'I do.'

They began to laugh. 'Hello, Annie,' he said. 'Isn't it a big adventure?'

His bus got entangled in the traffic below Fifty-seventh Street, and it was after ten when he ran into the Associated Press Building.

But the glass door of the news agency on the fourth floor was still locked and the empty corridor was silent. He paced up and down and thought, I wish I were a playboy. For one

31

year. I'd like to concentrate for a year on Ann Barbara Sevier, to the exclusion of all else. Then I'll be ready for service to humanity.

A sour-looking little man appeared and asked Philip what he wanted before he turned the key which he had already inserted into the doorlock.

'Did you think I was here to steal your damn bulletins?' Philip muttered to his back. Entering the office, he felt a heavy depression settling over him.

He sat down at a table pointed out to him; a moment later he heard the voice of the man with whom he had to deal, a stock Phillippine journalist called Tony. Tony came over and gave him a sheaf of telegrams. 'Here's the stock market,' he said. 'You'll get shipping after lunch, and the rest comes around four.'

'Good morning,' Philip answered.

Tony laughed. 'I never say good morning on Mondays,' he said. 'I'm not that much of a hypocrite. There's a whole stack of old news sheets on that shelf. Just follow the same pattern.'

Philip asked, 'Why can't we get our data before four o'clock?'

'Oh, the time difference, I guess. You're lucky if they are all in at four, anyway. Sometimes we have to wait till five or six, or even later – atmospheric conditions, you know.'

'Five or six!' Philip cried. 'But when do we get home then?'

'Well, don't forget you don't have to be in until ten, quarter past ten. When I handled your job I sometimes didn't get home till midnight. I had to do the mimeographing too, but we have a girl for that now.'

'That's just wonderful,' Philip said. I won't be seen dead in this place after six, he said to himself.

He put a sheet of paper into the typewriter and started, 'Manila Stock Exchange, February 21, Closing Prices.' At eleven I'll call her, he thought.

17

ANN was sitting on her couch, propped up in a corner with her legs crossed, and quickly drinking her Scotch.

'You have such silken legs,' Philip said.

She stretched out a leg to look at. 'Nylon,' she said.

'Ann,' he asked, 'tell me about your past?'

She played with her glass. 'I've known John for three years,' she said. 'I worked in Cambridge, in the Harvard School of Education, and I only saw him week-ends. I came to New York because I had finally decided to marry him,' she added with a little laugh.

'But you weren't in love with him.'

'I told myself I was.'

'And before him?'

'Before him – just some of the usual school romances. Nothing important. I was a very serious girl, you know. I scared boys.'

'Was John your first, your first man?' he asked hesitantly.

She laughed. 'Yes, he was. Is that awful? I was twenty-one, and innocent.'

'And then what?'

'And then nothing. I met him in Boston. He was just about to leave. We became friends – in a very calm way. I felt lonely, and he is very kind and considerate. Then after he'd gone to New York he started visiting me week-ends.'

'Is he in love with you?'

'He says so. Yes, I'm deeply sorry about it – it makes me feel guilty. I don't want to become happy that way.'

'Oh, Ann,' he said, 'he'll get over it. All's fair in love and war, and you told me – '

'I know,' she interrupted him. 'And we never made love the way you and I do – poor John, he didn't know much more than I. You must never be jealous of him. I'm not jealous of your past. I'm glad you are experienced – is that the word?'

'I'm an old roué.'

'Why did you pick me?' Ann said.

'Pick you! I found you! Do you realize I still can't believe that you really want me, that it is true? Don't you understand that you're the most perfect woman I've ever seen?'

'I'm not. You'll be terribly disappointed if you tell yourself that.'

'But you are!' Philip cried almost angrily. 'You don't know yourself! You have such a lovely body, and a spirit in it; do you think I'm one of those fools who think that some stupid movie star would be the answer from heaven? You don't know how furious that makes me, when it's implied that you may be happy with your girl or your wife, but of course it's just making-do – this whole ballyhoo that Miss So-and-so is the dream of all American men but obviously they wouldn't really know what to do with her if she walked into their bedroom; and so they settle for the girl around the corner – it's she who wouldn't know what to do with her 36–20–36 body. Look at their eyes! They're just dead dolls!'

Ann looked wistful. 'I'd like to be really beautiful all the same. Then I wouldn't bother to try and be clever either.'

'But you are beautiful. And on top of that you're alive,' he said pleadingly.

Then he asked, 'Ann, did you never have any side adventures?'

'Oh no. You were my first – except once, but that was only sort of.'

He looked at her, afraid she wouldn't go on if he made any comment.

'It was in Europe,' she finally said. 'Last summer. I was in Rome, and I met a friend, a colleague of mine from the Harvard school, and we . . .'

'We what?'

'Nothing, I've always liked him and we went out together, and things.'

'And made love?'

'Only once, only sort of. Oh, Philip,' she added in a different voice, 'don't be silly. Why do you pursue this?'

'I'm sorry,' he said. But he went on, 'Do you still see him?'

'Yes, I do see him,' she said, offended. 'We happen to work in the same place. We have lunch too sometimes. I won't any more if that will make you happy.'

'Yes it would,' he answered hoarsely. He shook himself and walked to the window. He felt half-sick. He looked out on to the street and said to himself, Stop it, you idiot.

18

LATER that week Philip moved in with Ann. It had been his idea; making the rounds of the dreary places offered for rent in the paper, he couldn't help thinking of her bright apartment. He had brought it up very hesitantly, although not because of his old ideas about privacy and how relationships flourished when you didn't see too much of each other. Those theories had now vanished from his mind. He hesitated only because he wasn't certain Ann would want it and anyway probably not so quickly.

But she had been quite pleased with the suggestion.

'Are you sure you don't want to wait and see a bit first?' he had asked.

'No,' she had said indignantly. 'I love you, you know.'

'How much is the rent?' Philip asked. 'I want to pay more than half.'

'Why more than half?'

'Because it's all your furniture.'

'Oh, for heaven's sake, don't be so difficult. I'll let you take me to dinner on pay day.'

His first week at the news agency, the hours had seemed endless each day. Yet when he received his pay cheque that Friday he somehow had the feeling that he hadn't quite earned it and that it was a lot of money for five news sheets. But he could not get away before half past six and that helped erase his guilty feelings.

Ann was waiting for him in the lounge of a restaurant in Rockefeller Center, and it was the first time he saw her looking cross. She didn't say much until she had had a drink, but then she smiled and said, 'I'm sorry, I was just hungry, and sitting here with everyone who comes in staring – it drove me crazy.'

'I apologize – I'll get out of that damn job soon.'

'It's a fine job. You mustn't pay so much attention to me. I'm treating to the drinks. Let's have another one.'

It became a wonderful evening; Ann took such delight in small things, he thought. She made their choice of restaurant and of dinner intense problems and yet she wasn't in the least a materialistic or trivial woman. 'I adore you,' he said to her.

She looked at him with a radiant face. 'Oh please do,' she answered.

They walked home under a freezing sky, and they both stood still in front of their house. 'You can see the stars,' she said, 'tonight they reach all the way to the sidewalk of Seventy-ninth Street.'

He put his arms around her and did a few waltz steps with her.

'I want to do so many things, Philip,' she said. 'I want to do gay things, and exciting things, and I want to do things for people. I want to go to India.'

'I want to make a movie,' he said, 'a gay movie, a musical, believe it or not.'

'Do you like to dance?' she asked. 'I love it.'

'I do too, Fred Astaire is a childhood hero of mine – but I'm terrible. Except when I'm in the proper mood. I'd want to make a musical which just sort of bursts at the seams – something very exuberant.'

'Oh, we will,' she said. 'We will do all those things.'

19

HE was lying next to her; she was still asleep. He stretched himself hard; he thought, what a lovely idea that we have a whole week-end ahead of us, that we can do what we want, within the castle of this apartment, no one can stop us, no one can see us. The city around us is like a vast shelter; its size and its indifference protect us.

This will last, because now at the beginning I am so very afraid of losing her, I am aware of the precariousness of my place in her life, I feel that she is literally too good for me. And that is a guarantee, for whenever I took a girl for granted in the beginning the time came when I wanted to move on again; it dawned on me that she could not be what the dream had been about. It was immature and egoistic, but –

Ann is a better human being than I am, her love is disinterested while I must have had all sorts of secret thoughts, what luck it was to find her and to live here, after being rather miserable and lonely in New York – but am I sure then that I love her?

Oh, all love is interested and disinterested at the same time; love is the only place where there's no conflict between these two. Perhaps that's even a definition of love? Ann said the grail wanted to be found. It is true that she was my find. I think falling in love and falling into love are almost the same.

All this seemed a discovery to him and he wanted to wake her. He turned and realized with a shock that she was lying wide awake and staring at him.

He forgot what he had wanted to say. 'You are the woman, Ann,' he said to her very solemnly, 'you're all womanhood. And you're lying next to me and no power on earth can come in between.'

'Would anybody want to?' she asked.

'Of course they would. People don't approve of pleasure

37

love. It makes them jealous. Love must be formalized, and burdened with all sorts of things.'

'Love should be more than bodies,' Ann said. 'I don't want to be loved like a woman in a Lawrence novel.'

'But it's not at all like that. That sex hygienist who thought that for passion you had to go back to nature, coal-miners and gardeners with deep roots in nature throwing ladies in the hay – it just isn't so! Love-making is a cultural achievement, honestly, Ann. Isn't it the only action where our bodies have got the better of nature, where we use them to express feelings and emotions? Savages don't make love nobly, they're much too busy fighting off animals and bugs and hunger, and they're always naked anyway. Once or twice a year they get themselves all worked up and then they have it and then there are the little ones next. Lawrence! He didn't know what it was all about.'

'Then you are still loving me for my body only,' Ann said.

'But there is no border line between your body and your mind,' he answered, 'it's all one.'

Ann laughed; his excitement caught her but made her shy. 'Will you teach me how to make love that way?' she said.

'You don't have to be taught, you know it all. It's not techniques, it's your spirit – you're the female pole of my world, your body is a whirlpool to drown in. I want nothing but that. You are the centre, here,' he said, touching her. He bent over and very carefully began kissing her body.

He looked at her. She closed her eyes. 'May I do that?' he asked.

She didn't answer for a moment, then she whispered, 'No one has ever done that with me before.'

'Please let me,' he said.

She put her hand behind his head and gently pushed it down again.

In the afternoon they went over to Grand Central Station to pick up a suitcase with Philip's books and papers which had come by Railway Express. He unpacked it on the floor of her apartment while she sat on the couch watching. He told her about each thing as he pulled it out; it got him involved in long explanations, but Ann insisted she liked to hear it all.

There was a manilla envelope with letters and photographs which Philip just flipped through. He put some of the photographs in a pile on top of the books. 'I want to throw the rest of this stuff away,' he said, holding the envelope.

'Oh, no, I don't want you to,' Ann said. 'It's part of your life.' She looked at him, she'd like to be contradicted, he thought.

'I want to get rid of it,' he said. 'Because I've found you. Because you are the one I have been waiting for.'

She took the envelope away from him and weighed it in her hand. 'But you've kept yourself busy while waiting,' she said, laughing at him.

He stood up and was going to answer, but seeing her face, he laughed too.

In bed and in the dark again, she asked, 'Tell me *why* you adore me?'

'Oh Annie,' he sighed, 'you're such a word girl.'

'I like that, being a word girl. What is it?'

'It's someone who lives in words. I can't say why I adore you. Because you're adorable.'

'Do you want to hear why I adore you?'

'Yes,' he said, but in that moment fell asleep.

20

'HAPPY Wednesday, Philip!' Ann shouted. It was their daily eleven o'clock telephone call. 'I saved that for now, I wanted you to be wide awake. It's our anniversary, it's a week ago.'

Philip was intensely pleased with this idea. When he had hung up he couldn't go back to his bulletin. He had to do something about Ann.

'I need a few hours off,' he told Tony. 'I promise you I'll get the bulletin out.'

Tony tried to look surprised but it was clear that he didn't care too much. 'That's crazy,' he said. 'You can't leave now.'

'It's an emergency,' Philip said with a smile.

Tony shrugged. Philip went back to his desk and called Ann to explain that he couldn't come over at lunch-time. 'Please don't mind,' he said, 'it's for a good reason.'

It had been snowing all night and when he came out of the building he shivered in his raincoat. He walked as fast as he could to Grand Central and caught an 11.25 train to Greenwich. The train was almost empty; its heat had the half-sickening smell of metal and oil.

In Greenwich a bright sun was shining on snow which was still white. On the way Philip had thought, perhaps I'm crazy; now everything seemed bright, easy, and obvious. He had the town hall pointed out to him and tramped down there.

'I want to apply for a marriage licence,' he told the girl at the window. He filled out a form and went across the square to a laboratory where a nurse handled the blood tests. 'You have to wait forty-eight hours,' they told him, 'you can come back any time after that. And your fiancée can have her test when you come to get married.'

Philip walked back to the little station with the receipt for the two dollars he had paid. There was no train for an hour and he sat in the waiting-room kicking his wet shoes on the concrete floor to get his feet warm. He kept taking out his receipt and looking at it, he felt very happy with that document; it was a tie between Ann and him, the first extraneous one. Of course it's nothing really, he told himself. I could have given anybody's name. But still, here we are together, in writing. I like that window with the grim clerk, and the nurse, and the matter-of-factness of it all. It suits. A blood test is just as romantic as pink champagne.

It was four o'clock when he got back to the agency and Tony looked sour. Philip finished his work as fast as he could, without even bothering to proof-read the stock-market prices.

'Several people will jump off roofs tonight,' he told Ann when she came to the agency at six, 'while a couple of others will finally buy their wives those mink coats. All because

40

where it says here Caltex 126 it probably should read 26, or 226.'

'Oh Philip, you can't do that,' she said.

He laughed. 'It's all right. Let's get the hell out of this place.'

She didn't ask him where he had been at lunch-time, so he finally said, 'Did you have a nice lunch?'

'Yes, I went with Helen, a girl in my department. That was a week-old date which I had kept postponing.'

'Poor Ann, your friends must be wondering about you.'

'They do or perhaps they don't. Not those who have seen you.'

She smiled at him. 'And you?' she then asked.

'I ...' He was suddenly worried whether he had done the right thing. 'I'll tell you about it later. I planned something.'

21

ON Saturday morning they were sitting in the kitchen drinking coffee. 'I feel terribly snug,' Ann said, 'I'm going back to bed after this.'

'Ann ...' he said, 'let's – I mean, do you want to get married?'

'Married?'

'Don't sound so surprised,' he protested. 'Don't women always like to get married?'

'I'm quite happy to live in sin with you,' she said.

'It's not that, you know better. It's – I don't know – I have the feeling that I don't want to spend another night in my whole life without you. And I want that formalized. I need a writ saying that I really got to Jerusalem.'

'I don't want to spend another night in my life without you either,' Ann said.

'That's where I went on Wednesday, to Greenwich Connecticut, to apply for a licence. I had been told about it. New

York, City Hall, is so crummy. We could go this morning, you know.'

She looked thoughtfully at him. 'I guess I would never want a formal wedding any more,' she said, 'not after cancelling one which was all arranged.'

'Well then.'

She laughed. 'I'd rather go back to bed. It's so nice not to have to go to that damn Foundation.'

He made a face. 'Suppose I ask John Gregg to lend us his car.'

'That would help,' she said.

'You're treating it all as a joke,' he complained. 'You think I'm making a fool of myself.'

'No, I don't. I think it's a sweet idea. But I'm yours already, you know – completely. Nothing you can do to make it more so.'

He kissed her and went to telephone John Gregg. The Gregg's expressed their dissatisfaction at not having heard from them for so many days but said they understood. John said Philip could have the car for the morning; Philip didn't say why he wanted it.

He hung up and came into the kitchen, but Ann had gone back to bed. He stood in the door and looked uncertainly at her. She began to giggle.

'Ann,' he said.

'I'm sorry – I'm enjoying this immensely,' she said, laughing. 'No,' she added, 'do go get the car, Philip. I'll get dressed. I want to go too now. Let's make it a party.' She jumped out of bed. 'Now I'm getting terribly excited about it,' she said.

There was the same girl at the window in the Greenwich town hall; she brought out the licence. 'What race do you belong to, miss?' she asked Ann.

'What race? Caucasian, I guess – isn't that the word?' she said, turning to Philip.

'She didn't ask me that,' Philip told her, 'It's because you look so wicked and dark.'

'We are Basques,' Ann said. 'That's why we pronounce our

name "Sevié". At least that's what my crazy aunt says she discovered.'

'Who's your crazy aunt?'

'She lives in Tennessee. She is a formidable woman straight out of . . .'

The clerk had listened impatiently to this and she now interrupted. 'You'd better hurry, folks. There's the test, and the judge leaves at twelve.'

' "Folks," ' Philip muttered.

They were married by a judge in a tweed jacket; he was going fishing afterwards, he explained. He lent Philip his ring for the ceremony; he often did that, he said, and it always brought luck.

'He looked terribly unjudgy,' Philip said when they were on the street again.

'He's probably a fraud. We're not really married at all.'

'Married – such a strange idea.'

'I'm not impressed,' Ann said. 'You got me on Tuesday evening and on Wednesday a week ago. But now I want rings too. We're going to buy them in New York. I'll buy one for you and you must buy one for me.'

'I've never worn a ring, I don't like rings for men,' Philip answered, 'but I do want to wear your wedding ring. Only, I have no money. I paid John Gregg back.'

'You can give me a post-dated cheque,' Ann said primly.

They bought two plain gold bands at a jewellery store on Madison Avenue. While Philip waited for the man to copy the data from Ann's driver's licence on to her cheque, she walked out. When he joined her, she gave him a bag to carry.

'I know it's rather corny,' she said in a shy voice, 'but I bought champagne.'

He smiled at her. She looked so young suddenly, and a bit lost; he felt a wave of tenderness towards her sweep over him, a wave of pity almost. I must protect her, he thought. I must never let her down.

'Oh, Ann, you're a dear one,' he said and he put his arms around her.

43

22

ANN had told Philip on the telephone that she was going straight home from work, and when he got there from the agency he found her laying the table with linen and silver. 'The Greggs are coming for dinner,' she told him.

'I didn't know you had such beautiful things,' he said in an irritated voice. He didn't want to see anyone; he felt the world, even old friends, a disturbance, an interference to them, and he had suddenly become anti-social. 'It's in your honour,' he had contended to Ann, who did not object to his attitude. And then there was this, Philip thought, he had really enjoyed going to parties only because of women, because of the chance and the challenge of meeting a woman; all that was over. And he felt vaguely that he would be jealous and uneasy in company with Ann.

'Well, they are your friends too,' Ann said.

'I know. I just don't feel like them.'

'I had to do something – I told John we got married.'

Philip made a face. 'I'm doing the work,' Ann said, 'so you have nothing to complain about. Just sit down and read the paper. All you'll have to do is open a bottle of wine for me.'

The Greggs arrived, very excited over the marriage, and bringing flowers for Ann; they made Philip feel ashamed of his lack of enthusiasm. But he didn't quite come out of his isolation and mildly annoyed Ann by following her around and into the kitchen for whispered conversations.

Only when the Greggs were leaving did he feel so relieved that he finally became warm and friendly. He escorted them to the front door of the building and there John said, 'if you want our car next week-end you're welcome; we're staying home. It looks as if we're finally going to get some half-way decent weather.'

'Oh, that would be wonderful,' Philip said. 'Thanks a lot.'

He got the car on Friday afternoon and drove over to the apartment to pick up Ann. He double-parked and rang the bell twice to let her know he was there. Waiting, he jumped up and down the steps to get warm. He looked up at the clear green sky, which was rapidly withdrawing in the twilight. A spring sky, he thought ; it tries to suck you up into it.

Ann came out a moment later carrying her over-night bag. 'That's fast,' he said happily.

'I was waiting,' she said, 'I'm terribly pleased. It's exciting.'

As he slumped more comfortably into the seat and drove up First Avenue as fast as he could in the rush-hour traffic, he felt pleased too. She sat close to him, and pointing at another car said that she didn't understand couples who let children, dogs, or parcels sit in between them.

Philip just looked sideways at her and smiled. It felt nice to be driving a car again, he liked driving with her next to him. It's such lovely freedom, he thought, I wish we had everything we own in the back, and some money, and we would drive on, anywhere.

'I like the way you drive,' she said. 'Are you happy?'

'Yes, I'm happy.' And after a moment he went on, 'You know, since I was a child I have been dreaming of cars and of roads – the promise of them, and the endlessness. Well, I have been twice across the U.S. in my own car and once by bus, once hitch-hiking – I've driven in Europe – but this is the first time in so long that I feel that same excitement again.'

'Is that because of me?'

'No, it's because John Gregg has such a gorgeous Plymouth.'

'Oh.'

They smiled at each other in the rear-view mirror.

Philip took a deep breath. Some burden – the apartment, the news agency, the Greggs for dinner – had vanished. They were back in the purity something has before it really begins. 'It's a splendid thing we got away,' he said.

'I'd love to travel with you. We must go to Europe as soon as we can manage,' Ann answered.

And then they were on the parkway going north, darkness had fallen, and the oncoming cars became a roar of stabbing headlights.

23

THEY ate a late dinner in a roadside restaurant; they joked about the awful menu under the eye of a disapproving waitress.

Afterward they had a drink in the bar. The light there was dark red; a jukebox in a corner added yellow, white, and green. They took their glasses and stood in front of it and played songs. She sang softly with some, in a very deep voice. 'Jesus, Ann, I love you,' he said in an undertone.

Outside, the sky had clouded over; far to the south over the city it was lit up in a yellowish haze.

As they got back into the car, a fine drizzling rain began to fall. The roar of the parkway now changed to a swish. In the beams of their lights the rain seemed to be sucked towards them in bundles. 'It looks as if someone were pouring it from a watering-can,' Philip said, 'the way they do in a movie studio to imitate rain.'

Ann, who had talked busily before, had fallen silent. Thus they drove on, with few words. 'Do you want me to drive?' she asked.

'No, not unless you'd like to. I'm fine.'

An hour north of Albany they drove into the darkened entrance of a motel. A very old man appeared who showed them a room. It was nice, with dark wooden panelling, a polished wooden floor, red curtains, and bedspread. 'Swiss Chalet,' Ann said. 'I'll turn up the heat a bit,' the old man told them, 'and there's an electric fire too you can use.'

Philip followed him to his office to pay, and when he came back Ann had turned off the overhead light and switched on the fire. 'Let's sit in front of it,' she said, putting a blanket on the floor. She went into the bathroom to undress, and then she installed herself, leaning against the bed, in the red glow. 'Turn off the table lamp too,' she asked him.

He sat next to her and she looked at his body, she caressed

his chest with her left hand and then let her hand glide down
and hold him. He wanted to stroke her too but she shook her
head, 'you just sit there,' she said, 'I want to worship you a
bit tonight.'

He trembled.

'Are you cold?' she asked lightly.

'No, I'm not cold, Annie,' he said. 'I'm trembling because
I'm dying. You're a goddess. I would love to be sacrificed to
you.'

24

'IT'S awful, going back,' Philip said as they entered the city
along Bruckner Boulevard on Sunday night. 'Isn't it straight
out of the inferno?' he asked, nodding at the Bronx apartment
houses rising darkly behind the line of neon-lit roadside shops,
used-car lots, and gas stations.

'It isn't pretty,' Ann answered. 'But you mustn't fight it. Just
ignore it.'

'But it seems all so anti-love.'

He drove her as fast as he could to the apartment and then
he took the car back to the Greggs.

'Sorry to have been so long,' he said to Ann when he re-
appeared. 'Gregg asked me in for a drink and I couldn't say
no. He was alone and looked sort of miserable.'

'It's all right, it gave me time to make supper.'

Philip slouched into a chair. 'Gregg had all sorts of advice
for me about marriage. How we shouldn't lock ourselves up
so, and that it was dangerous to be too intense. Marriage was
a compromise, and a working relationship, and all that stuff.
I was furious.'

'Oh, poor John,' Ann said.

'Why can't he leave us alone? Even if he's right, that's no
reason to spoil our time now.'

'He doesn't mean to spoil it. He can't anyway, Philip. I

47

don't feel a bit like a compromise girl with you. I feel as if I'm waving a flag.'

'He just doesn't know,' he said, 'he doesn't know that you are a unique woman. I used to believe that business, how marriage wasn't designed for happiness but for society. I thought I'd never want to get married. I still think a man can ruin a woman by marrying her – not by not marrying her, as they always have it in novels.'

'Then what made you change your mind?'

'You!' he shouted, suddenly feeling happy again.

Ann laughed. 'All those novels must have done something to our minds. I remember as a girl how relieved I always was when marriage was safely in the bag. You felt that after that nothing really terrible could happen any more to the heroine.'

'And you could see how right they were. Naughty girls always got in the family way at the first throw.'

'What awful language, Philip,' she said.

'But it's so. That's in English novels, of course. In French novels the girls could go on for ever without even giving it a thought.'

'I guess I am glad I'm living in this century. We have some things to be grateful for.'

'Yes, that's terribly true,' Philip said, almost surprised. 'I hadn't thought of that, really. It's science that has freed woman. Love has come truly into its own with the invention of antipaste.'

'What!' Ann said.

'Like antipasto. My private word for contraception.'

'You're terrible,' Ann told him, going to the kitchen.

He followed her. 'I'm just joking,' he said.

'Me too.'

'I'm glad you told me that about this damn century. It does give it some compensations. That and dentistry.'

'Aren't you happy living now?' Ann asked.

'Oh my God, no.'

He paced back to the street window. 'I would have liked to live in the Middle Ages,' he said, 'or in Athens, or anywhere – but in a time when the world was still young.'

48

25

THE following week-end they went to Brookline.

It was crowded in Grand Central Station; Philip didn't say much until their train was moving. 'I realize it's high time I made an appearance there,' he said then. 'But I must admit I hate it.'

'My parents are very sweet,' Ann said gently.

'Your parents couldn't be anything but sweet, Anne-Marie,' Philip said. 'Look at the product they made. But I'm just nervous about it. I hate family affairs – and after a rather grim week with oil and plantations and stocks and bonds –'

'I like most of my names,' Ann said. 'I'm not sure I go for Anne-Marie.'

'Anne-Marie is a German waitress in a mountain inn. You look a bit like one this evening. I'd love to pinch you.'

'That means I'm getting too fat,' Ann answered. 'Let's go have a drink in the club bar. You'll get a late but beautiful dinner when we arrive.'

They looked out at the wasteland of New York in the wet twilight. Trees, houses, puddles in the fields stood out sharply. There were the first cars with their headlights on. An abandoned fairground loomed up in the darkening rain. 'Amusements of America', it said on a truck parked beside a dripping iron shed.

The meeting turned out to be less difficult than Philip had anticipated. Ann's parents were at the station with their car; and there followed such a bustle of greetings and talk about plans, shopping, friends who wanted to see them, that he could hide in the general commotion. Once seated in the back of the car on their way to their house and half-listening to the conversation, he thought that they did this perhaps more or less on purpose, to put him at ease, and he felt very warm towards them.

Ann's father was a rather short, dark man; her mother,

thin, with greying auburn hair, looked very English, he thought. She might have been pretty once, but neither of them had the looks which could let you expect them to have a beautiful daughter.

'It's a long drive, Philip,' Ann's mother said. 'We live in the suburbs. Ann must have told you.'

Ann, who sat in front with her father, turned around and put her hand on his arm for a moment, as if to delineate their belonging together.

They were shown up to their bedroom, which was Ann's old room. 'You might be cold here in the night,' Ann's father said and he started showing her where to look for blankets.

'Yes, yes, Daddy.' Ann pushed him more or less out of the room. 'We just want to wash up now, we'll be down soon.'

She closed the door behind him and turned around to look at Philip. 'So this is it,' he said and smiled.

'Yes, this is it. This room is about twenty years of my life.'

'Seventy-five hundred nights,' Philip said.

'Is that what it means? That doesn't seem so much.'

'There aren't much more than twenty thousand nights in a lifetime,' he remarked. He walked over to the bed and looked at a print hanging over it. It was an old-fashioned gravure; a lady in a hoopskirt was shaking a stalky apple tree for the benefit of a little girl. 'Souvenir de Mortefontaine' was printed in the script underneath.

'I like that,' Philip said, and he sat down on the bed which squeaked.

'It's not a very good bed,' Ann told him. 'You'd better get ready to go down for dinner.'

'Please stick with me,' Philip asked, 'don't leave me alone to make conversation.'

'You'll do splendidly,' Ann said and vanished into the bathroom. She reopened the door on a crack and added, 'My mother has already told me that you're very handsome.'

WHEN they were up in their room again later, Philip felt ill at ease. I can't quite take these sumptuous dinners, he thought, wine, liqueur, cigars – not my style. 'I'm just a country hick,' he said to Ann, 'I'd do better on a poor-boy sandwich.' She didn't listen to him, 'Please lie next to me,' she said. She looked glowing and excited. She bent over him to kiss him on the mouth and waited for him to make love to her. He knew he did not want to, but he made himself go through the motions; then he became increasingly aware of the recalcitrance of his own body, of the noises of the bed. He lay still, listening to the sound of washing up in the kitchen below, and his strength ebbed away. He moved off her and she turned her back towards him without saying a word.

After a long time she said, 'Let's go for a walk.' She got up and put jeans on, her sweater, sneakers, and a raincoat; he felt weary, but he didn't want to refuse her and he dressed too. They left the house through the back door into the dark garden.

They came out on to the road, the wet concrete softly gleaming from the light of the high lamp-post at the corner. Last year's leaves still covered the pavement on the side of the road with a brown film. Their steps were almost soundless; at the first crossroads he took her hand.

'It's the equinox,' he said.

She looked sideways at him; he could just see the pale reflection of her face.

'Spring has begun,' he explained.

For a moment he could see a star between two ragged clouds.

'I have walked this street so often,' Ann said. 'Every day, when I went to high school.'

'Were you a happy child?'

'Oh yes, I think so. Often, anyway.'

'I have seen you walk here,' Philip said. 'I have dreamt of

51

this street, of walking it with you. I have been here before, in my dream.'

'At times I believe in fate for you and me, in our being destined . . .' She did not finish her sentence.

'I do,' he said.

They went back to the house. He took off her clothes for her and came to her. He remembered for a moment and then forgot how things had gone wrong earlier. They were in a rhythm suddenly imposing itself; the bed, and all else, was silent now. Each coming deeper into her was like a step, he vaguely thought; it was like that walk along the dark road. And when she sighed, he had her so deeply that it hurt, a pain, a lovely pain, he said to himself.

27

'YOU slept so hard,' Ann said to him the following morning, 'I listened to your heart-beat. I was frightened.'

'Why?'

'It is such a little sound. We're such fragile creatures, I thought of you dying one day, and it all seemed so sad, so desperately sad . . .' She had tears in her eyes.

'Sweetheart,' he cried, 'please don't be silly!'

'Don't you think it's sad? I wish I didn't love you so.'

'Oh, Ann,' he answered, 'you mustn't be afraid of life – isn't it better to live and . . .' He interrupted himself. 'You know what,' he said, 'I do believe the principle of the universe is couples.'

Ann looked questioningly at him like a child waiting to be reassured.

'There's really no reason why our species or any species has to propagate itself by love-making,' he said to her, 'you could just as well conceive of a world in which every being was on its own, had its own offspring, the way microbes do or whatever they are – loneliness could be the principle of nature, but it is not, it's love-making, it's becoming one – we won't be alone when we are dead, we will be one –'

Ann felt better now and she didn't want him to go on, 'Eternal togetherness,' she grinned.

That morning they sat in her room and in the basement and she showed him the contents of all closets, drawers, and boxes which had a connexion with her. He looked at high-school yearbooks and her college blazer; he saw photographs in which she was a dark solemn child, a girl on a pony, a spindly fourteen-year-old, and finally an immensely attractive girl, in a white bathing suit sailing in Canada, or looking very gay and carefree in a group on a Roman square.

'My God, how buxom you look there,' he said.

'I gained fifteen pounds in Europe. It was a hard job getting back to normal.'

'But it suits you – who are all these people? Is he in it?'

'Just acquaintances. No, he isn't. There is no "he" anyway.' She wanted to take the photograph away but he held on to it. 'I want to keep it,' he said, 'may I? You look so wonderful in it. Please stay that way. Don't let me make you all serious and adult and married, please.'

There was also her childhood diary in a notebook. 'I didn't keep it for very long,' she said. After some pleading on his part she said he could read it but not with her present.

He went outside and sat on a folding chair in a sudden bright March sun. He read about her favourite place in the garden, which was a hollow between two trees growing together, and about the glories and miseries of parties and dances for which she could or could not have a new dress. Most of it though was very serious; Ann had already then been concerned, concerned with people and the world. There were wild ups and downs of happiness and despair in the notes. They ended abruptly in the middle of a page written after she had said good-bye to her best friend, who was moving to Washington. Two girls, they had solemnly shaken hands in a clearing in the little woods near by, and then each had walked away without looking back. Only at the edge had they waved once.

It all seemed to fit; it flowed into one image for him with her ex-libris, the gravure over the bed, their first night, the champagne she had bought after Greenwich; and it made him feel again that he had to be protective, that she had a right to be shielded by him against the wrong things of life, against the bitterness of disappointment.

28

THEY had met for lunch at a counter on Sixth Avenue. This was one of a series of places where they had their lunches, roughly half-way between Rockefeller Center and Ann's Foundation. These ranged from French restaurants on down, according to their financial situation of the day. It was the end of the month and Philip had discovered that he had just about enough cash to pay his share in the rent for April and no more.

They ate hastily, with people standing behind them, their coats in their laps and trailing on the floor. 'It's too damn hot in here, let's get out,' he said. They walked north along the avenue, past buildings being torn down and steel skeletons for others growing; it was a meagre spring day, clouds racing across the light blue sky, dust and newspapers flying over the sidewalks.

'I'd love to be in nature now,' he said. 'Think how beautiful Manhattan must have been two hundred years ago.'

'But I like it now, too,' Ann said. 'I like the capital-of-the-world feeling it has. Don't you feel any of that?'

'Yes, I do. I guess I want to have the best of both worlds. But it's such a stone lump. If only there were more trees. I like to shuffle with my feet through dead leaves. It's good for the soul.'

They entered Central Park and found a hill which sheltered them against the wind; they sat down on the short brown grass.

Ann took her suit jacket off and put it behind her. She lay down on it, put her coat over her legs and looked up contentedly at the sky. 'When it gets warmer we can eat sandwiches in the park,' she said lazily. 'Philip, tomorrow I'm supposed to have lunch with some people from my office.'

'Oh.'

'Do you mind?'

'Are they male or female people?'

'Both,' Ann said. 'But don't worry. My main topic of conversation is usually my husband.'

He made a bow in her direction. 'And what will they talk about?'

'Shop of course. And the girls about clothes. The men about their families.'

Then she said, 'Perhaps I'll want to have a child some day.'

'Oh no,' Philip said.

'Why not?'

'I don't see myself as a father. I don't like family life.'

'You're exaggerating,' Ann said.

'My parents divorced when I was a child – I must have told you. I lived with my mother, and people always assumed I missed a lot – "it's so bad for the children" and that stuff. But I was content. When I stayed with a friend and I saw Father come home and sit around in his shirt sleeves and give orders, and the whole household revolving around him, I thought it was awful – so, so middle-classy.'

Ann sat up. 'While you were upper-class?'

'No-class. I prefer that.'

She lay back again. 'But don't you think that people who love each other –' she began, dissatisfied.

'Should have children? I think love-making serves its own purpose – when you start doing it for some other reason, for an extraneous reason, to have children, it changes.'

'You are exaggerating,' Ann repeated.

'Don't you believe that we should try and live our own lives first? That we admit some kind of defeat if we start shifting our hopes and ideas to "the next generation"? Which will do the same, and so on and on, *ad infinitum*?'

'I agree with that part of it,' Ann said. 'I don't like that either. When I see some of my college friends, bright girls who had all sorts of plans, things they were going to do, work, think

– and next time you see them they are all bogged down, stringy hair, junior screaming, another junior in the make, and their conversation consisting of baby food and rashes. . . .'

Philip laughed.

She asked, 'Tell me something – what do you feel when you make love to me?'

He thought about what to say. 'What do you feel?' he said for an answer.

'Oh, many, many things,' she said quickly. 'I think our love is a star and I feel its brightness. I feel empty and you fill me. It makes me whole. We're one, and every time you're with me that is reaffirmed.'

He looked at her.

'That was a sweet look you gave me,' she said, 'why?'

'Because you're such a holy girl,' he answered.

29

LATER that spring they bought a car, a second-hand convertible. Ann had the money for the down payment in her bank account, and he was to pay the monthly instalments; they agreed that they couldn't really afford it but they wanted it all the same. It was a white car with blue leather interior, and four years old – 'the last sensible model', Ann considered. The first time they drove to Brookline, Ann's father gave her new tyres as a present. They now had to be even more money-conscious, and Philip again began to canvass around for a better job. Ann deserves to have nice clothes, he thought, and to be taken out to the theatre and places. He wanted that too and he wanted another place to live.

I'm getting more and more grey-looking in this city, I need some sunshine, he told himself. And I don't want to make love to Ann with always the noise of planes overhead, neighbours playing their blasted T V sets and flushing their toilets.

Philip had developed a system by which he parked their car just before ten in the morning on Park Avenue and retrieved it at noon to pick up Ann. After lunch he cruised around in the Sixties until he found a parking space; if all else failed he bribed the doorman of the Associated Press Building to let him leave the car there. At lunch-time they drove over to Sutton Place and ate sandwiches on a bench beside the river.

On most days Ann was home first, even if she walked or took the bus. Usually she didn't start making dinner; she waited for him. They had come to have a drink together when he got home, to talk a bit until the infringements of the day and of the outer world were taken care of, and to make love.

Their days then turned around the idea of passion, of the desire they felt for each other. They never planned to make love; it happened, and it meant very much to them that it was so and that love was not something which could be delegated to the end of the day after teeth-brushing and turning of bed covers.

'My ideal house has two different types of bedrooms,' Philip said, 'bedrooms for sleeping and bedrooms for making love.'

He then told her that Japanese noblemen in the nineteenth century used to maintain two houses on their estates, one for the husband, one for his wife, and that they asked formal permission of each other for every visit.

'I'm not impressed,' Ann said. 'Does that appeal to you? I wish I'd cured you of your idea that marriage and love are enemies.'

He hesitated. 'But I think you have cured me,' he said, 'but that's for us only. I'm not thinking about us. I feel we are above the law.'

'And what's the law?'

'Well, I don't think love and marriage go together like that horse and the carriage – like two horses perhaps, if they agree with each other you go very fast, but if they start biting and kicking you end up in the ditch.'

'I think it's so simple,' Ann said. 'When you have made love to me I want to fall asleep in your arms. When I wake up in the night I want to feel your body near me. That's love too.'

57

30

SHE appeared to him the outcome of a long search, years of waiting; he liked to think about their meeting and marrying in wild terms, stars, destiny, the knight reaching the holy city. How could he safeguard these ideas in the dailiness of life? He dreamt of a desert island for them, a real one, with silence and aloneness.

'I want to lie naked on a beach with you,' he said. 'Not once but for weeks and months. I wish you could promise me a year like that, somewhere, sometime.'

'We'd get terribly restless after a while,' she said.

'I wouldn't. Oh, women – they're supposedly so romantic, but they're not.'

'But I am,' she protested. 'And I feel able to carry my romance out, right out into Seventy-ninth Street. It needs no shelter.'

'Oh, but of course it does!' he cried. 'All worthwhile things do!'

31

THEIR favourite bar was a place on Third Avenue with a clientele of bums, working men, non-working men of un-identifiable tendencies, and a sprinkling of the rich. John the bar-keeper was a thin Irishman whose very unamused manner lent a kind of dignity to this setting.

Philip and Ann took a table next to the jukebox and he went to the counter to get their drinks. 'I love all cafés,' he told her. 'In Europe, in Paris, I once spent twenty-four hours on end in a bar.'

'Let's drink to us,' Ann said, hooking her hand with her glass around his arm and bringing it up to her mouth. Philip had to stand up to reach his own glass. A man at the table across from them coughed contemptuously at this. 'Shut up,' Philip said to him.

'Please, Phil, no scenes,' Ann said while inspecting her face in her pocket-book mirror.

'Isn't it terrible,' he grumbled, 'how people hate any manifestation of love or joy – how they squash everything out of the ordinary. That's what's so wonderful about you, you're uninhibited. You're part Latin of course. Northerners are really for the birds.'

'I thought I embarrassed you sometimes with that uninhibitedness,' Ann observed.

He was taken aback by her knowing that. 'No, that's different. It's very complicated.'

'Everybody loves a lover,' sang Ann, who wasn't taking all this very seriously.

'It isn't so!' Philip said. 'They do at the official moments, at the wedding, for then it's all leading directly to increased sales. But outside that frame, nix.'

Ann smiled at him. 'You're in a terribly crusading mood these days.'

'You mean I'm a bore,' he said apologetically.

'You under-estimate normal day-to-day love, tenderness, a family like my parents for instance.'

He didn't answer.

'Let's play songs,' she said.

He got up and put a quarter in the jukebox, made his selections, and sat down with a grin on his face.

'Why do you look like a cat with a canary?' Ann asked.

'They have "From This Moment On" and I pressed that three times.'

'You mean – oh no, that won't work,' Ann said. 'At least I hope it won't.'

'Oh yes it will,' he told her. 'I also put it louder, you can turn the volume screw with a dime; it's just around the side, at the back.'

'If I'd known you were a juvenile delinquent,' Ann said.

John came out from behind the bar and angrily turned the volume down again.

'You and I babe we'll be riding high babe from this moment on,' Philip sang to her as the jukebox began to play the record for the second time.

32

ANN read from the Sunday *Times*: '"House on hill, no neighbours, $125 a month." Sounds too good to be true,' she said, 'there must be something terribly wrong with it.'

'Where?' he asked.

'Ardsley. It says, "Twenty minutes from Manhattan" and it gives a phone number. It also says "closed on Sundays".'

'Thank God,' Philip sighed. He was lying on the couch, reading, and hadn't felt at all like doing anything else.

Later Ann said, 'I will call Monday morning.'

'If it's a good place, it will be rented by nine a.m.'

'Well, let's go there at eight then.'

They did get up the following morning when the alarm rang, and at half-past eight they were in Ardsley. Ann went into a gas station to call and get the address and they drove over.

The road climbed a hillside; there was a gate at the top and here the real-estate man was waiting for them. It was a splendid house, they both thought immediately. 'A bungalow,' the man said. 'The owner got transferred.' He led them around and introduced them to the owner's wife. There was a grass field all around from which miraculously no other house was visible. 'I used to take sun-baths here,' the lady of the house said.

They trailed behind. 'Let's take it,' Philip said. 'We want the house,' Philip told the agent. The man laughed. 'When we put that ad in,' he answered, 'the boss said you'll have a busy day. I had eight or ten calls before I even left the office.'

'But it is available?'

'You're the second party to see it. One lady has been here, but she wasn't sure. She'll decide today.'

'Do you have to wait for that?'

'Yes, I promised. But I'll take your application. You're a nice young couple – no children? You can give me a deposit if you want to. I'll call you as soon as I hear from her.'

Driving back to Manhattan, Philip said, 'That blasted woman who couldn't even make up her mind on the spot. I'm sure she'll grab it ahead of us.'

'It's really terribly expensive for us, you know. It would be a hundred and fifty if you add it all up.'

'Oh, Ann, it's such a wonderful place, so quiet and sunny – everything would be so different. Perhaps that fellow expected some kind of a bribe?'

When Philip talked to Ann on the telephone at five that day, the man had not yet called her. He decided to call Ardsley himself, but the real-estate office was closed.

That evening Ann planned how she would arrange her furniture in the house. She was now carried away by the idea too, 'I have the feeling I'll never be happy again if we don't get it,' she said as they were lying awake in the dark.

'Oh, what nonsense,' Philip protested but he felt almost the same.

He called the agent again the following day at noon, after having postponed doing so all morning. 'Oh yes,' the man said. 'I'm terribly sorry, that lady did take it.'

'She did? When?'

'Yesterday – yesterday afternoon.'

'Why didn't you call us?' Philip cried indignantly.

'I mailed you back your deposit cheque, with a note.'

Philip hung up without answering.

33

THE head of Ann's department at the Foundation invited them to a party. 'Laura,' Ann told Philip. 'You've met her. I introduced you once at lunchtime when we came down together – a very tall girl.'

'Laura? I think I remember – sort of gawky-looking.'

Ann shrugged. 'She's nice, I think she and I will become quite good friends.'

'Do we have to go?'

'But I want to go! I like parties – I thought you did too. She has a huge apartment at Eighty-second and Park Avenue. She's terribly elegant, you know, Social Register and that kind of thing. But she's sweet.'

While he dressed for the party, Philip was decidedly unhappy with the way he looked. The beat generation, he said to himself, ten years later. The car-sick generation. 'Ann,' he called, 'I look awful.'

She came out of the bathroom to look at him. 'But how on earth can you put on a green tie with blue socks and brown shoes?' she said.

'I know. But there aren't any other socks.'

'Why don't you wear the blue tie my father gave you?'

'I don't like ties with figures on them.'

'Well, something's got to go,' Ann said, going back to finish her make-up in the bathroom mirror.

Only when he took off his raincoat outside Laura's apartment did Ann see he had kept on his green tie. But just then the maid opened the door for them.

They entered and Laura came out to greet them. 'What a lovely dress, Ann,' she said. Ann did look very smart, Philip thought, she was such a party-dress girl. Laura welcomed him and then took Ann along to the bedroom; Philip was left standing alone at the edge of a crowd of guests. He made his way through them to the bar which was set up on a long table and asked for a Scotch which he drank without looking at anyone.

Soon after Ann came and took him over to a circle of people. 'This is my very brilliant husband,' she said gaily, and Philip felt embarrassed, for her rather than for himself; he was struck by the idea that the others did not fall in with her exuberance and thought her a bit silly. Ann started to tell a story; they're not listening very hard, he thought.

He drifted away and went back to the bar.

After a while he began to wander through the rooms; and came upon her standing alone in front of a book-shelf with a cigarette. 'Ann,' he said surprised, 'let me get you a drink.'

'All right, I'll come with you.'

'I hope you don't want to stay too long,' he said when they had struggled away from the bar with their glasses, 'it's not a very inspiring gathering.'

He said that to console her but she looked sharply at him, and he added, 'Well, you don't seem to be having such a wonderful time.'

Ann made a defiant face, a bit bitter. 'I'm not a very popular girl,' she said, raising her eyebrows.

'Oh, now you're just being silly,' he answered, working his way back to the table with his empty glass. He turned around to take hers too, but she walked off.

Later while drinking brandy from a tumbler and listening to a college professor explaining Fulbright scholarships, he caught sight of her at the far end of the room, talking very animatedly and intensely with a young man. He felt a pang of jealousy. It's not fair, he thought, Ann needs self-assurance and I, the man who loves her, can't help her with it. Not all she needs. Is it the same for a man? Would I like for the women here, for one woman, to know that I'm a good lover? He frowned at himself, to the annoyance of the professor who muttered something about a refill and turned away.

34

THEY took a taxi home because Ann said she couldn't walk another step in her dress shoes. They waited what seemed to him an endless time at a red light. She saw on his face that he was about to hold forth on the party and she said quickly, 'Philip, please, no married-couple post-mortems about my or your or anyone's behaviour. I'd scream.'

He was taken by surprise but didn't say anything after that. They were both rather drunk.

At home, Ann put a flamenco record on the phonograph and then, without paying any attention to him, kicked off her shoes and began to dance. She danced well – there was nothing self-conscious or amateurish about her, Philip thought. What a strangely dualistic woman she is. If those party people could see her now –

Ann started taking off her clothes while dancing; he looked hard at her but she never looked back at him. When the music stopped she turned off the record player, went into the bedroom, and lay down. He came in and made love to her; she very much used him, and she fell asleep without having spoken a word.

In the middle of the night Philip woke up. The desk lamp in the other room was still burning; he got up to turn it off. He picked up Ann's clothes from the floor and put them on a chair. After that he lay awake for a long time. He felt unaccountably sad.

It's really not too easy sleeping in one bed with somebody else, he then thought. I wonder whether she'd mind changing this for twin beds.

35

'ARDSLEY' became a byword of frustration for them; for weeks afterward they bought the *Times* late on Saturday nights and drove all over Westchester and west Connecticut on Sundays, but they never found anything like that house.

It was a spring of wet week-ends.

'It's rich man's weather,' Ann said. 'I'm sure tomorrow morning the sun will be shining out of a clear blue sky.' They were sitting on the bed, the Sunday paper spread all around them. The rain made dirty streaks on the windows. It was so sombre outside that they had the lights on.

'I wish somebody would phone,' Ann said.

He made a face. 'We used to cover the telephone on Sundays.'

'That's why no one calls me any more.'

'The honeymoon is over,' he concluded.

'Oh, Philip,' Ann said angrily, 'because I don't want to lose all my friends? If it's over, it was over when we had our first fight.'

'But we haven't had any fights.'

'You have shouted very loudly at me.'

'I always shout when I get excited,' Philip said. 'It doesn't mean anything.'

'It does to me,' Ann answered, 'but let's stop this nonsense.'

But he decided to go on. He realized that he shouldn't, but he couldn't check himself from jumping up and saying, 'I'll go for a walk, why don't you call your friends in the meantime.'

When he came back an hour later, wet and tired, Ann was standing in the doorway of the building.

'Ann,' he said, 'why are you standing here?'

'I was scared. I ran after you and you had vanished. It's a frightening feeling not to know where you are.' She was trembling.

'Oh, I'm so sorry,' he said, leading her to the elevator, 'I'll never do it again.'

'We must promise never to go off without letting the other know where we are,' she said when they were back upstairs.

'I promise.'

'It frightens me that people who love should ever shout, or try to hurt each other. It's such sacrilege. I'm sure we'll be punished for it.'

Philip shrugged and smiled at her.

'Phil, let's start a new period tomorrow without any more fights.'

'Yes. And without you calling me Phil.'

'I want to make a calendar with a red cross for each fightless day. If we have a whole week I'll take you to dinner at Le Pavillon.'

'And if we don't, I'll take you there,' he said.

'Now let's cheer up,' Ann said, 'this is going to be a nice day after all.'

36

SUDDENLY the wet spring came to an end and almost overnight the city was blanketed with summer heat. 'I know it's a bore to talk about the weather,' he told her, 'but you must admit, in this city of yours it's damned hard not to.'

They were having their daily eleven o'clock telephone conversation.

'It's so hot in here, already,' he said, 'that the Asian news bulletin feels it has never left home.'

'I feel terribly smug,' Ann said, 'I'm on the air-conditioned floor. One above me they're miserable too.'

'Tony, why aren't we air-conditioned?' Philip shouted over the partition.

'Tida ada wang,' Tony shouted back, 'which means: no money, boy.'

'You don't mind.'

'Oh yes I do. Manila was never like this.'

'He says Manila was never like this; neither was California,' Philip said in the telephone. 'Think of San Francisco right now, all grey and foggy and damp.'

'Come and have lunch in my office,' she suggested, 'you can sit here and cool off.'

'That's a sweet idea. I will.' Philip put the receiver down and stared ahead, then focused on the sheet in his typewriter. He added another word to the sentence he had been at when Ann called, and then he leaned back in his chair.

After a while he went over to talk to Tony. 'When can I get some vacation?' he asked him.

'You haven't been here much more than three months.'

'It seems three years,' Philip said.

'I know this is no job for you. And not for me either. This is a lousy place,' Tony stated unexpectedly.

Philip looked at him. 'I wouldn't dare agree.'

'You will when you've been here as long as I. Why don't you try the United Nations?'

'Not a chance, I've been told.'

'You can always try. I'll ask the boss about vacation. I'm sure you'll have to wait till fall, at least.'

The lobby of Ann's building enveloped him in coolness. Ann was sitting at her desk, and he sat opposite her. 'You always look so incredibly efficient here,' he said.

She pulled their sandwiches out of a drawer. 'It's all sticky and slightly revolting,' she said.

'Ann, I asked for a vacation.'

'They refused of course.'

'Yes. But I want to go all the same. I'll wangle a week.'

She looked up from her efforts to separate two slices of cheese.

'I got road maps at Esso on my way over here,' he said. 'I want to drive to Canada.'

Ann's face lit up. 'I'd like that.'

He unfolded a map of Canada and put it on her desk.

'Look here, Anna, isn't it a wonderful sight, all this

whiteness? In that country the roads just end in the middle of nowhere; you know, I could look at it for hours. I can't think of anything more exciting than places like this,' he added, pointing at a name on the map, 'a town at the end of a road, at the very end.'

37

THE fourth of July would be on a Thursday, and Tony informed him that he could have that week off, though with loss of salary since they would have to hire someone else. He accepted, and all of June he went through the days just waiting for the month to end. He felt feverishly restless but tried to make the rides Ann wanted to go on, evenings and week-ends, as short as possible: he had a premonition something would come in between and prevent them from going to Canada, and the most obvious disaster would be their car breaking down beforehand.

They were both nervous and weary. Ann had stopped trying to achieve her calendar week of fightless days: sequences of red crosses were regularly broken off by a fight. They went into long analyses afterwards and she usually took most of the blame.

But as long as the atmosphere had not cleared, Ann would not make love.

'Subtle feminine blackmail,' he once said which made her very angry. 'For your information, a woman is as interested in love-making as a man,' she answered. 'But I just don't feel like being intimate with an enemy.'

'I could never be your enemy,' he answered softly.

On the last Friday in June Philip worked in a frenzy and was through at a quarter to five. Five minutes later he was at the Foundation where Ann fell rather limp into the car. They drove until midnight; once across the Tappan Zee Bridge it had quite suddenly become cool. They took turns driving, both going fast. He spun fantasies for himself about their being fugitives from the police; he enjoyed the idea and thought up ways of crossing the Canadian border unseen.

The following day at noon they drove into Montreal; at five o'clock they reached a little town called St Donat.

This was the name at-the-end-of-the-road which they had decided on. A lake was just north of it and the road led towards it beyond the town.

'You're disappointed there's still more road,' she said.

'Christ no, this is wild enough for me.'

The asphalt had ended before the town and the road was only a dirt track now, with ruts and big stones which crashed against the bottom of the car. They passed tourist courts but they bumped on, 'Let's try a bit longer,' he kept saying. The road reached the lake and then came to a farm where it really ended. A thousand feet farther a little wooden house was standing in its own garden near the water. 'Look there,' she cried.

He went to the farm and came back to tell her that the cabin was available for twenty dollars a week. 'And they'll bring firewood,' he added. 'But it's very primitive – wood stove, oil lamps, no running water.'

They went to look at it. 'I don't need running water,' Ann said, 'and neither do you.' 'True.' 'Let's take it.'

'It's such luck,' she said, 'it was really waiting here for us, and it is the end of the road. It's getting dark too. We just made it.'

He went back to the farm to pay and then took the car bumping across the grass to the house.

38

THE house at the lake was the closest they ever came to his idea of a desert island. It was an entity, for the fact that there was no gas, water, or electricity gave him a consciousness of insulation, of absence of links to the world. I'd much rather always pump up my own water and light oil lamps, he thought, than be forced to live at one of the couplings in the web spread over the earth by man. And when they saw a human being near their house they knew that he was heading towards them and no passer-by; he could only be someone from the farm bringing wood or eggs or other food that was for sale there.

The lake made an inlet into the little wood behind the house, and there a rowboat was moored. Blueberry and strawberry bushes grew up the walls. It was all very wild and green and thorny; 'It's something out of a children's book,' she said. 'It's the most wonderful house I've ever lived in,' he answered. Nothing broke the silence during the long days but the cries of birds overhead. At the edge of the water an outhouse had been built. After dark Ann made him stand guard when she went there – not too close, but not too far either; she was afraid of the bats and other creatures which made unidentifiable sounds around the house all through the night.

They had a big bed, partly built into the wall and of wood as was everything else. On it they piled all the blankets and rugs they could find, because the nights were very cold with gusts of freezing wind blowing through the cracks in the walls. They had a very simple and basic kind of love-making in this bed – the old-fashioned kind, he thought; in the deep dark, completely buried under blankets, it seemed to him like something out of Laurence Sterne. 'Steam heat must always have been the enemy of warmth,' he said.

They rowed out on to the lake, taking turns at the heavy oars and the steering. It was a big flat boat, hard to keep going over the weeds and branches that obstructed the inlet. They called out navy-style commands at each other while working their way through. Once out on the lake they let the boat drift; there was very little wind between the high shores.

Around them mountains filled the horizon; the light vibrated over uninterrupted slopes of pine trees, as in the primeval world.

39

ONE afternoon they rowed all the way to a far sand bar jutting out into the water. The air was hot, and they lay on a blanket on the sand, taking turns at chasing away the big flies.

'Think of all those novels with juvenile seductions staged around swimming in the nude,' Philip said. 'You really have to be pretty sophisticated for outdoor love; wouldn't you say teen-agers fall into the trap in cars and on couches with plenty of clothes to help them along? I don't believe a male or female virgin would feel any special temptation just by taking off a wet bathing suit and getting sunburned and bitten all over instead of only in parts.'

'Would you?' Ann asked, laughing.

She stood up and took off her bathing suit.

'Take off yours too,' she said. He did; he felt his heart beating wildly.

She lay down and stared hard at him. 'It's a lovely idea that I do that to you,' she said, 'you take my breath away.'

'You mine.'

'Don't mind the flies,' she whispered in his ear. He kissed her on her mouth and did not answer.

They fell asleep under their blanket and when they woke up the sun had dipped behind a band of loose clouds over the western horizon. Long vague shadows fell over the water which was patterned with trails as if drawn by an invisible boat. It had grown cold.

They sat up and blinked at each other.

Philip got to his feet. 'We'd better start rowing and get warm again,' he said peevishly, trying to swallow. His throat felt parched. He pushed against the bow of the boat.

'Oh, not just for a minute,' she asked. 'Do you mind sitting here a moment longer?'

'I'm sorry, I thought you were freezing,' he answered.

She did not listen to him but stared out over the lake. It was very still.

She said hesitantly, 'I had a feeling of discovery, discovery of what life and we are about – I suddenly loved you differently from any love I've ever felt before. As if you were me, but more than me. . . .'

He pulled her up and put his arms around her.

She took a step backward and said, 'I want to remember this feeling. I want to remember it always. Let's give this beach a name. It's the most beautiful beach I'll ever be on.' There were tears in her eyes.

He looked at her but did not say anything; they stepped into their boat.

A hazy light was coming down upon them; the air was almost unbearably pure.

She said, 'I'll call it everywhere beach.'

40

On Saturday morning they had to go home. 'I've never had such a nice one-week vacation,' she said. 'It was more than that, it was more than a nice vacation,' he answered. He felt deeply depressed, and he was afraid of the future.

They didn't bother with packing, but just put their clothes in the back of the car and weighed them down with the cans left over from their one foraging trip to the town. The farmer's wife came to the gate and shook hands with them. 'And now it's really over,' he said to Ann. 'You mustn't be childish, New York isn't that bad,' she said.

He had asked her to drive first and he was leaning back, with his head towards the sun and his eyes closed, looking up only when she had to brake.

'Don't you think we should sleep in Canada?' he asked. 'The motels are cheaper here.'

'We might as well get as far as possible. The traffic will be wicked tomorrow, after the Fourth of July week-end.'

He groaned.

They crossed the border late in the afternoon. Abruptly the landscape changed; the European empty road became a highway, isolated from the houses and fields along it and with clusters of cars materializing out of nowhere. The bill-boards appeared.

'If we can hold out for cheap gas we can afford a decent restaurant,' she announced after counting their money. 'I'm not up to diners tonight.'

'Me neither. Would you mind terribly driving again after dinner? I'm just not with it.'

She drove for a long time after their dinner stop. It was a dark evening; he sat huddled next to her, dozing, starting every now and again from the fierce reflection in their mirror of the lights of a car coming up behind them. Nightmarish clusters of neon signs loomed up, arrows jumping on top of gas stations; chickens, pigs, and frankfurters in yellow, pink, and blue; revolving lights looking like distress signals: all silently crying out as they flew past.

He sat up when she turned sharply into a motel drive-way. 'Let me handle it,' she said, 'you're very tired.'

They had a room with twin beds. 'I guess I'll get straight into my own bed,' she half asked him, 'you do look dead on your feet.' He smiled weakly at her.

She lay in the dark, and then a sound from his bed made her turn towards him. She put out a hand and touched his face.

'Philip,' she said, 'but you're crying!'

'I'm terribly sorry,' he muttered in his pillow, 'I know that's a disgusting thing for a man to do – I don't think I've cried since I was ten years old.'

She got into bed with him and put his head on her shoulder.

He bit his lip but his body still shook. 'I'm terribly sorry,' he repeated, 'I don't know what's the matter with me – '

'Oh dear, oh poor dear,' she said.

'I do love you,' he whispered.

41

ON their first day back in New York Philip came out of the Associated Press Building at lunchtime and stood still on the sidewalk. The weather was brilliant, under a dazzling but cool sun the people walking and sitting around seemed happier and better-looking than ordinary; it was a city day.

He was on his own, for Ann had a lunch date. He leaned against the balustrade beside the Rockefeller Plaza fountain; below him the restaurant tables were laid with fluttering checked table-cloths. He stared fascinated at an extremely well-groomed man who was sipping a drink and talking to two girls, one on each side of him, while a hovering waiter tried to adjust the umbrella over their chairs. He had a sudden yearning to be part of things too, as he imagined that man to be; your name in gossip columns, your photograph in the magazines – I know it's all vanity, he said to himself, but I'd prefer tasting it and then rejecting it over my sour-grapes rejection.

He began to walk east as quickly as he could through the noontime crowds, and on First Avenue he cut across to the United Nations Building. Without stopping at the reception desk he went up to the Personnel Office and told a secretary clutching a sandwich that he was interested in a job in the news department.

'The Department of Public Information,' the girl corrected him in a high French voice.

She looked doubtful when he asked whether he could use the typewriter on an empty desk to fill out the forms she had given him; he managed a self-assured grin at her and then sat down without waiting for her reply. When he cursed softly because of a typing mistake she offered him her eraser.

After he had filled out the application he went to the office of the World Health Organization on the twenty-second floor, to F.A.O. in the same building, and later across the street to the headquarters of the American Delegation to the United Nations.

All that week Philip used his lunch hours to make the rounds of agencies and foundations handling news and political matters.

'Why don't you have a go at the advertising agencies?' Ann asked him one evening.

'Oh, I want to stay in news if I can help it,' Philip murmured, brooding over one in his series of romanticized curricula vitae.

When all the applications had been mailed in, he found that he could not suppress a feeling of expectation, a birthday-morning idea of something nice is going to happen. He announced aloud that it was all hopeless and that he had just done it for the hell of it, but he nursed a vague image of a job in Geneva or Rome, with a house on a hill and Ann walking in a garden, a maid laying a white table on the terrace, everything fresh and new for them. Evenings when he came home he thought, There just might be a telegram – it is possible – 'CAN YOU REPORT FOR WORK ON SEPTEMBER 1 TRANSPORTATION YOU AND YOUR WIFE NEW YORK ROME PREPAID CABLE ANSWER COLLECT SIGNED FAO.'

But no such telegram ever came.

42

PHILIP dreamt that he was walking along an embankment in a tropical city; there were houses and a row of lamp-lights reflected in the dark smooth water. The air was as soft and as sweet as night air can be only in a hot country, 'I've never seen this place except at night,' he said, 'that's why it seems so romantic to me.'

He came past a house with a balcony along its second floor and saw a young woman step out on to it. In the diffused glimmer of light it was just possible to see how lovely she was. She looked out and up at the sky, as one might before going to bed, and she said half-aloud to herself, 'I hope it won't rain tomorrow.' Then she went back inside.

He stood still and looked at the façade of the house over the black water.

A young officer walked by, a man he had been to grade school with as a boy. He recognized him immediately. Brown, he thought, we used to call him Brown, as a first name. Brown was wearing an Air Force uniform; he looked very dashing. He greeted Philip with a warm smile and a lifting of one hand as he went by.

I wonder whether he knows the girl on the balcony, Philip thought.

And then he woke up, and he tried to hold on to his dream.

He felt as if all longing, all hope were buried in it, all expectations of long ago. That was my youth, he thought. When you are young life has that glitter, the glamour, which means magic, of the unknown.

How could I ever love a real woman, he thought, as I could love that girl on the balcony while she looked up at the sky and felt the wind on her face and wondered about the rain?

43

HE counted off the summer days and nights in the city one by one; he was waiting for autumn, and each day lived through became a small victory. You can't lock out the city in summer, he said to himself.

I used to like the feeling of all those houses and people around us. It feels different now, turned against me; it's because I am no longer a Californian but a New Yorker. New York is polite only to her guests; she's a cannibal eating her own kind. It's a war almost.

He was still embarrassed at the thought of having cried the

last night before they were back from Canada ; and he did not talk about this idea of inimicality.

One evening they were lying next to each other on the bed, late, the window open to a humid wind. They were facing each other ; he kissed her on her mouth in an endless kiss ; she shivered from it. A radio started playing at that moment. It was not very close to their apartment but the quality of the sound showed that it was turned up very loud.

He lay back.

'What is it?' she whispered.

He waited a moment, then he jumped up and put his clothes and shoes on. 'Those bastards,' he said.

He went downstairs and later she heard him walk in the courtyard of the building and shout at somebody.

When he came back to the room the noise had stopped.

He listened. 'Did it stop? I'm afraid it's pure coincidence. There's a fence across the yard – I couldn't get near the place.'

'Sit here,' Ann said and put one arm around his neck.

He withdrew. 'Just a sec.,' he muttered and vanished into the bathroom.

When he finally came out, Ann had installed herself on the couch with the book she was reading. She didn't look up.

'Are you mad at me?' he asked after a while.

'No, should I be?'

'Are you sure you're not angry?' he asked again later.

She put her book down. 'Well, if you insist, Philip – I didn't like the experience of a man recoiling when I try to embrace him.'

He stared at her. 'Oh that,' he then said. 'I didn't recoil – I had been running across that yard, looking for that damned radio maniac. I felt sweaty and repulsive, that's why.'

She shrugged and looked probingly at him.

'Love in this city . . .' he began.

She smiled. 'It's all right,' she said. 'You're all right.'

And then he thought, You can only be happy in this city if you accept it ; you can't fight it.

Why do we stand it? Why don't we break up and go, since nothing is more important than love? Why is there something unreal about people who vanish to Tahiti or a Sicilian fishing village?

Perhaps because they lack courage. It's like going into a monastery compared to the asceticism within-the-world of those tough old Protestants. But if that's what love does, finding your true love is in a way an ending of living –

44

It had been his longest day at the news agency yet, with the last cable coming in at six. It was past eight o'clock when he left the silent building. 'Nice evening', the man in the night elevator said without taking his eyes off the control panel.

Outside it was already darkening. A warm wind played between the high building of Rockefeller Center. Philip had protested to Tony about unpaid overtime, but now he did not feel indignant at all; he was in no hurry to go anywhere. He walked across to Fifth Avenue to get a bus.

He saw a Number Four coming up the avenue and got on; he walked to the back and as he sat down the driver switched the bus lights on.

Why did riding a bus with the electric lights on affect him so suddenly?

There was something strangely stirring in it, the dusk outside, the bright light on the faces of the passengers – something saddening and intimate; it made him think of the living-room in the house of his childhood: the large overhead lamp with the round silk shade was lit, it was after dinner, he was doing his homework at the table; a rising wind brushed the branches of a tree against the windows. His mother, his mother and his father were talking softly on the couch. Then it must have been long, long ago, he thought, I must have been a small boy; the homework must have been something else –

Soon it will be autumn now, he said to himself.

A girl across the aisle, not really pretty but very young and studenty, with straight hair, was reading *Bonjour Tristesse*. I know why so many people have read that book, he thought, it has the fascination of hardness. The millions and millions who sit at their empty wood-burning fireplaces and face wives or husbands they don't love or even like, dream of such hardness. They wish they could free themselves too. Loneliness holds them back, fear of loneliness. Sometimes tenderness.

They look out of the window and dream of the highway but all they can see is the reflection of the room in the glass.

He looked across at the reading girl. If I were still a student, he said to himself, I'd stay on. I'd get off where she would get off, I'd start talking to her, she would end up by asking me in and fixing dinner for us.

The girl had become aware that someone was studying her and she threw an irritated glance around before returning to her book. He hastily looked away.

He grinned. This is not Portland, he thought, in New York she'd call a policeman.

But his mind returned to his last image, in which they were eating spaghetti, he in a chair, she cross-legged on an old couch. She would let him stay; and there was her narrow bed, the old pyjamas she'd wear, and waking up late in the morning and rather shyly drinking coffee with her.

When he got home he surprised Ann, she had expected him to arrive tired and cursing the news agency, but he embraced her and said, 'I didn't mind, sweetheart; it was just a chore that had to be done. It couldn't be helped. I'm so glad to see you. Oh, Ann, please let's not drift.'

He wasn't asking that of her, he was asking it of himself.

45

IT was half past five; he was typing the last sheet of his bulletin when he heard Ann's voice in the office next to his. She was talking with Tony.

He stood up and looked over the partition. 'Ann!' he called, 'why are you here?'

They turned towards him. 'Back to work, boy,' she said, 'I won't speak to you till you're finished.'

When he was through he hastily handed in the last sheet and went to get Ann. He nodded good-bye to Tony and whisked her out of the office.

In the elevator she gave him an amused look. 'What is the matter with you?'

He frowned. 'I wonder what you found to laugh and chat about so animatedly.'

'Tony told me that ...' she began, but seeing his face she changed her tone and said, 'You're a bore.'

When they were on the street he took the direction towards Fifth Avenue, towards the car; she walked next to him in silence. After a while he started again. 'He's a friendly chap. But I've always thought his conversation was rather limited.'

'Who's friendly?' she asked distracted.

'Tony!'

Ann turned her head towards him. 'You mustn't judge people so hastily,' she then said. 'Tony is quite interesting if you come his way a bit.'

Philip couldn't say why the idea of Ann and Tony laughing together irritated him. He fell silent again.

When they had reached the car which was parked on Fifty-eighth Street, he said, 'Do you want to drive or shall I?'

She hesitated a moment. Then she answered, 'You haven't asked me why I came to your office.'

He felt tempted to say, 'To flirt with Tony perhaps.' He gave her a victimized look. 'I did ask.'

'Oh well, now it is all spoiled anyway,' Ann said. 'Here you are.' She gave him a small envelope with two theatre tickets.

'If you'd rather not go, say so. I can take you home and go with Laura,' she said.

'That's fine with me,' he answered and got into the car on the right-hand side.

She started the engine but then he put his hand on her arm. 'I'm sorry, sweetheart,' he murmured, 'I'd love to go with you. Please forgive me.'

'Oh Phil,' she said very sadly.

'Please, please forgive me,' he said. 'Nothing has happened. It's only six o'clock.'

'But you don't know. I had it all planned. We were going to have dinner first, near the theatre. I didn't want the car. You've made me walk ten blocks in these shoes – look.' She lifted her foot.

'Ann, don't be upset,' he said hastily, 'we'll take a taxi back from here, I'll pay.'

Ann drained her cup of disappointment. 'It was a surprise for you,' she said almost in tears, 'because it's the twentieth of August, our six-months anniversary.'

'Oh, you are a sweet girl. I never thought of that. Come, you'll see, it will be all right.'

He jumped out of the car and ran to the corner of Fifth Avenue. He stood out in the street and waved vainly at the taxis streaming by.

Suddenly he felt as if he had broken something valuable, something he would never be able to make whole again.

46

SUNDAY-MORNING breakfast; a hesitantly starting late-summer day. Ann was reading the theatre section of the *Times* and he was staring at the politicians on the front page of 'The

News of the Week'. 'Ann,' he asked, 'let's go for a walk in the park.'

She looked at him in surprise, for he always announced that he couldn't jostle his way through all those papas and mamas airing their off-spring on week-ends in Central Park. 'All right,' she said, 'let me put my slacks on.'

He walked her through the wet grass to a hill and they sat down on a newspaper. 'It's going to be a good day,' she said, looking up at the sky, where patches of blue were breaking through.

'Anna Karenina – ' he began, and stopped.

'Throw yourself under a train,' she finished for him.

'No, listen, Anna. You've locked yourself up sort of, of late. You've built a shell around yourself.'

She turned her head sideways. 'Perhaps,' she then answered, 'one has to, at times, not to get hurt. Perhaps you did the same.'

There was an undertone of defiance in her voice. He hastened to say, 'Of course, I understand that. You don't have to defend yourself, I'm not attacking you. I just wanted to say, you shouldn't be afraid of being vulnerable, because no one is out to hurt you. I could never hurt you, Anna.'

She now gave him a very warm smile. She is such a nice woman, he thought, when I really try, she comes across too. 'And so,' he said, 'I wanted to come here, and I want us to say that we'll shed our shells and trust each other.'

'It's too early. You must wait for Easter,' she said.

He kissed her.

She laughed at him with half-closed eyes. 'I'm game,' she said. 'This is a shell-breaking ceremony.'

47

IN the lobby of the Associated Press Building Philip, hurrying because he was late, was hailed by a loud voice. Turning, he saw a friend of his from the *Los Angeles Times*, a heavy man called Robert Murray, waving at him.

'Hello, Philip,' Murray shouted. 'How's New York treating you? You're a bit pale.'

'No swimming-pools here, only cess-pools, ha, ha,' Philip muttered. 'And what are you doing in New York?'

'I'm here for the United Nations General Assembly,' Murray said.

Philip looked impressed. 'I didn't know you people believed in foreign policy.'

Murray laughed. 'Oh,' he said, 'there's always the juicy piece on how the taxpayers' money goes to buy Martinis for the Ruskis – that kind of thing, you know.'

'I have to rush,' Philip said, 'but how about you and me having a Martini?'

'Fine. Today? I'll be at the press bar in the UN.'

'I'll come over.'

In the elevator Philip smiled. Murray, with his Machiavellian soul and his childish face. He was pleased. I'm completely out of touch with things, he thought. Good old Los Angeles.

When he talked to Ann at eleven he did not say anything about his date; he thought that he would rather go alone, but he didn't quite know how to handle it. At five he called her and after a moment's hesitation said he would be late because of a drink with a journalist – there was an interesting job possibility in it, he said.

When he entered the bar Murray was there and immediately pushed a Scotch towards him. 'Drink up,' he said, 'we have to hurry.'

'Where to?'

'Drinks and dinner at the Overseas Press Club.'

'Oh,' Philip said disappointed, 'I can't go.'

'Why not?' Murray asked while waving at the barman for his bill.

'Well, Ann would – I'm married, you know.'

'No!' Murray cried delighted. 'Then why didn't you bring her?'

Philip shrugged and drank his Scotch.

'I bet she's too pretty to bring out,' Murray laughed. 'You

old fool – you don't think she's home knitting while you hang around in bars?'

'Of course she's home knitting,' Philip said, 'we're not as modern as you and your wife.'

'Touché,' Murray cried. 'But I wouldn't want my Nancy to be knitting, I want her to have a good time.' He climbed off his stool. 'Call your wife,' he said, 'and tell her to hop a taxi and come over. Tell her Uncle Murray wants to inspect her. Wait, I'll give you the address of the club – it's not far from here.'

He started searching his pockets and interrupted himself to look at his change brought over by the barman. 'Two more, but very fast,' he said.

'No, I don't think she'd . . .' Philip said.

'Oh come on man, what do you have a wife for? Is she pretty or isn't she? What are her vital statistics?'

'She is pretty,' Philip said stiffly.

'Well, there you are. I'll point out some big shots to her, and if she makes a hit with one of them, it might lead to something – hell, you don't think jobs are distributed by personnel managers, do you? They're distributed with cocktails. No point in a young man marrying if it doesn't further his career.'

'I guess I'm not that practical,' Philip said. Of course there is some truth in what the man says, he thought. But Ann would scream if she heard this kind of talk. She makes me feel different towards Murray, inimical – he used to seem so amusing once. That realization made Philip annoyed with her.

Murray had suddenly decided to desist.

'Can I drop you somewhere?' he asked when they stood on the street.

'I'm going uptown,' Philip said, 'I might as well take the First Avenue bus.'

'Give me a call!' Murray shouted as he climbed into a taxi.

A moment later Philip was standing alone at the bus stop, rather drunk.

48

PHILIP and Ann had thought that John Gregg and his wife were at odds; they had not heard from them for a long time. Then Dorothy asked them to dinner. No one spoke about the past months; and John and Dorothy were very tender and warm with each other.

Philip was pleased. 'Of course, one shouldn't be too intense,' he announced to the Greggs, thinking of John's marriage theories, 'marriage is just a compromise, you know, and a working relationship.' John remembered and laughed. 'That was the counsel of despair,' he said. 'And what is the counsel of hope?' Ann asked. Gregg puckered his forehead. 'Hope needs no counsel. That's a quote from Marcus Aurelius,' he added apologetically.

Everyone was very much himself, and it was a gay dinner. Ann's basic seriousness is in place here, Philip thought, it is like that first lunch of the four of us. It is possible to have things this way; it is possible to be a couple without having to turn your back towards the world.

They left late in the night but they felt wide awake and walked along the parapet along the river to look at the moon; the cold little waves of the East River threw back its light in sharp reflections. 'Do you think moonlight is romantic?' Ann said.

'Oh no – it's much too frozen.'

'Yes, it's a cold light. Even in the South. It almost frightens me sometimes.'

'I wonder who ever started calling it romantic. Perhaps that's from the days when people necked only at night.'

She laughed. 'And now?'

'Well, now you have for instance movie houses,' he suggested.

She said, 'I think human beings must have been most happy

85

on earth when they realized there *was* a mystery but they could not even begin to fathom it.'

'Most afraid, I'd say,' Philip said. Standing there beside her at the river, he felt suddenly very aware of their own uprightness in the light night; it seemed a discovery. 'Men are the only aerials,' he said, 'the only straight creatures on earth. We're aerials, to receive the truth.'

'Wow,' Ann said. 'What about herons?'

'Herons too. But herons look down all the time, they're watching for frogs. Men look up, every now and again.'

He could not sleep that night, and he got out of bed and sat on the window-sill. The moon had set below the houses; a low roof opposite him was just barely silvered still by its light. In the east the sky was already not quite dark any more.

Then, all at once, he saw himself on the earth. He saw himself sitting on the sill, in the house standing on the surface of the earth; the earth revolving, slowly lowering his own particular horizon until the rays of the immobile sun could catch its edge and shine over it. The world turning, and he felt as if he knew all its secrets, as if there were so few – he and his fellow passengers on this small planet, how simple it would be to captivate them, to let them know that you knew their secret and your own, that you could tell them of their life and death, that they would recognize these and be moved. How simple and confined it was, to tell the story of the world to its house guests.

There is but a limited number of us, he thought, a limited number of destinies and emotions. If you draw lines between them all, then that pattern is everything, all stories, all tears, all laughing.

In the east a long thin line of cloud reflected colour. He felt as if he had come upon a great truth, as if salvation was within his reach but he could not say yet how. I must regain control of my life, he thought dimly, I must leave my shelter.

49

ANN no longer held herself away from him when they were in conflict about something; she had become very demanding. An impersonal element seemed to have entered her desire. She wanted to experiment, and she made him caress and kiss her body for long times. It made her wildly exciting for him; her body remained the dark mystery, and this intimacy was breath-taking and almost unbelievable. The very idea of a woman desiring so seemed to him enough to make a man go mad.

But they were separate in this. When she made him come into her at the last moment only, it was over for him so quickly that he underwent a terrible shock of transition; making love, which had just before blacked out the whole world for him, disintregated suddenly into nothing. He lay beside her in silence, with closed eyes, and felt set upon by a dark melancholy.

'Are you happy, Philip?' she asked him.

He hesitated. 'Yes,' he said.

She laughed a bit scornfully almost, he thought. 'You don't sound very convincing,' she said.

'Well, it's a tricky question. You'd have to define happiness first.'

'Don't be difficult,' Ann protested.

'What made you ask the question?'

'Oh, I don't quite know,' she answered softly. 'We have gone through a lot of struggles – I have made someone very sad – I'd like to know whether it all added up to something, whether I have succeeded – whether I've made you happy.'

He couldn't bring himself to say the easy 'Yes, of course you have.' 'Perhaps the only happiness is in the search for happiness,' he answered.

50

Robert Murray invited him to a party, 'very wild, lots of terrific women', and Philip accepted. He did not try to leave Ann out of it again; perhaps I can make her see his amusing side, he thought. But when he brought it up she began to laugh.

'I can see in your face how you'd love to go alone,' she said.

'Oh no, Ann,' he protested.

'But I understand perfectly. Every man must want to play the bachelor again occasionally.'

The idea of going alone had seemed attractive, but less so now. Ann said, 'I think it's very wise not to be old-fashioned about these things. And I have a party too on Friday, of the Foundation. You're invited of course but you'd be bored to tears. So it all fits beautifully.'

She seemed so relaxed and natural that Philip said, 'Well, I guess you're right. It's very sweet of you to take it that way. I would love to mess around a bit the way he and I used to. Not with girls of course, I don't mean that at all.'

For a moment he thought he could read in her face that she was hurt by his acceptance of this plan, and he was about to ask her whether she was being honest. But then he quickly decided to leave well enough alone; she couldn't hold it against him if he took her at her word.

On Friday evening he first drove Ann to her party in the Eighties; she had insisted that he keep the car since he had to go down to the Village. She looked lovely, he thought; when he had taken her to her destination he hesitated and began, 'Ann, are you sure you don't mind?'

'Oh, for heaven's sake, Philip,' she said and walked in without another word.

He stared after her. Finally he got back into the car and drove off.

Robert Murray received him with much noise and friendliness and Philip said to himself, Oh to hell with it all; why should I be a hypocrite. In the end everyone tries to do what he or she really wants to do and nothing else.

So he let himself be taken around and introduced by Murray as the most eligible bachelor in New York, 'But your bachelor wears a wedding-ring,' a girl said. 'He thought this was a fancy-dress party,' Murray answered, 'he came as me.' They all laughed about this.

The 'lots of terrific women' boiled down to one or two, Philip discovered, but it was a wild party: exactly the kind of evening Murray used to produce in his house in the Hollywood Hills. It was amazing how he had been able to make the same sort of people gravitate towards him in New York. There was nothing very special or different about it all, but it made Philip feel free and exhilarated; just because it puts me back five years in time, he thought.

Later in the evening Murray, very drunk, sought him out to talk about the happy times.

'A sure sign of getting old,' Philip said, 'all those nostalgic looks of ours at the past.'

'Of course, my boy, of course we're getting old. But don't think I'm going on much longer with this kind of nonsense. I'm not that stupid. Soon my wife and I are going to calm down, and settle down, and raise a family.'

Philip looked at him, and he thought Murray's face was haggard and tired. Poor man, he said to himself, I don't think your marriage will last that long. I hope it works out for you.

And then of a sudden he didn't feel amused any more, nor the need to be amusing. He felt a bit above it all. Ann and I are really doing better than all these frantic people, looking for they don't know what, he thought.

Murray had vanished again in a crowd. There was no need for formal good-byes at this stage; Philip hastily slipped out of the house.

He hurried to the car; it seemed very important now to get to the other party before Ann had gone home.

'Come on boys, come on,' he muttered through his teeth at the red lights on Fifth Avenue; he jumped ahead as soon as the cross-street green went out and counted the blocks he could make – thirteen per light. North of Forty-second Street he had to slow down somewhat, but he drove in less than ten minutes to the house where Ann had her party; he was very sober suddenly.

The door of the apartment stood ajar; the sound of voices steered him to it. He walked in and stood on the threshold of the living-room but did not see her. 'Damn,' he said.

But then his eyes fell on her, standing in a group near the window. She turned her head towards the door in that same instant, and as she saw him her face lit up in a radiant smile.

51

AT the News Agency Philip found a letter waiting; it was Ann's writing. For a moment he was wildly astonished and thoughts flew through his head about her having left him, the apartment empty.

'I think there is a bridge between love (as passion) and marriage (as fulfilment),' she wrote, 'a bridge between the one full of tension and the other lacking in tension. I can't find a better term for it than tenderness. Tenderness is composed of lots of things – of love for a person out of all that you have shared and share, love for their oddities and irregularities as well as purities, a dash of pity (you may not approve of this, but I truly believe it's essential – pity in the sense that the whole human race is on occasion to be pitied – not pity as a general attitude), and above all: compassion, feeling with a person, not looking at them. Not seeing a situation only as you see it, but as that person sees it – so if he or she is frightened by something, you don't just say, "silly, how can you be scared?"

'These things carry us through life, make love not a beautiful fireworks display but a lot of strong candles burning brightly through the night.'

He put the note down. It's a sweet letter, he thought.

It is pleading – that time I was so ironic because she hadn't dared ask for a raise – but when I scream it's because I can't bear the thought of the world getting the better of her. I fight the world because of her or for her, and she jumps in between.

His thoughts wandered. Oh, we don't have to be so serious, he told himself ; we burden things too much.

He put his hand on the telephone to call her, but it rang just then. It was NBC; they told him they wanted a news report for their education programme and would pay him a hundred dollars for it.

He put the receiver down and thought, I want to do something crazy, I want to break the routine we're caught in.

He dialled Ann's office. 'Ann, thank you for your note,' he said happily.

'Oh?' She was a bit surprised at his reaction.

For a moment he doubted his own mood but then he said what he had planned to say: 'Annie, I have a plan and I'm sure you'll like it. Let's meet after work in our bar – I don't want to go home. Then I'll tell you all about it. And let's be cheerful please, for everything is going to be splendid. Just you wait and see.'

52

SHE had gone home first to change and came to the bar half an hour after he had got there.

He hardly waited until she sat down to say, 'We're going to Europe.'

'You're mad.'

'I've figured it all out and it's possible.'

Ann looked bewildered.

'Suppose you bring me a drink first,' she said.

He hastily went over to the bar and came back with a glass of rye. She drank it all and put her glass down with a sigh. 'All right now,' she said.

'NBC called me, they want a ten-minute report on the new grade-school crop. And they'll pay a hundred dollars for it.'

'Yes?'

'That hundred dollars will pay off the car. Which means we can sell it. We can buy another one when we get back, and I'm sure we'll get seven or eight hundred dollars for it. If we leave six weeks from now, and live on only your salary for that time, we'd have another four hundred from me. That makes eleven hundred. With the four hundred you still have, fifteen hundred. That's enough for three months in Europe and cabin-class boat to and fro included.'

'And our jobs?'

'You told me that old Foundation of yours give unpaid leave.'

'I expect they would, but what about you?'

'I'm sick of my job. I'll get a better one when we come back.'

'But all those months here that you've tried –'

'That's because I didn't really have to,' he interrupted hastily. The more he thought about it, the better the whole plan seemed to him.

'Have you heard from that Murray yet?'

'No, what does he have to do with it?' he asked, surprised.

'But you told me he knew of something for you.'

'Oh yes, that. No, I haven't heard anything,' Philip answered, blushing. He had forgotten that he had thought that up to make his drinks with Murray sound more legitimate; it had been the first time he lied to her.

Ann looked at him, 'Well, anyway,' she said, 'I guess you're right, if you have to, you'll manage.'

'And we can sub-let the apartment,' he went on, 'six weeks will give us plenty of time. We'd be away before winter – we could go to Spain or Sicily or Greece.'

'It sounds divine,' she said, but she sounded less enthusiastic than he'd thought she would be.

'Think of what you'll miss – sleet, and rain, and the whole jazz of Christmas shopping – we'll save a hundred dollars right there.'

She laughed. 'I like Christmas shopping,' she said. 'But what if we can't sub-let our apartment?'

'Of course we will. A place with a ceiling rent, it will go in a day.'

'I wouldn't mind giving it up,' Ann said thoughtfully, 'and selling the whole lot. I'm rather fed up with it anyway.'

This went too far for him. 'You don't mean that,' he said, 'all your splendid furniture.'

'You can have it. Can we afford another drink on this budget of yours?'

'Oh yes!' he shouted. 'Ann, you are willing then?'

She held her head sideways and gave him a look which seemed odd to him; it was as if she were trying hard to find the answer to a puzzling question which was just outside her reach.

'Yes, I think so,' she said, 'but can we brood over it a bit longer?'

53

HE escaped completely into his Europe plan; he felt it would solve everything, it was their desert island; they'd come back with fresh eyes, he said. 'It's really feasible to live on a hundred dollars a month for two in Europe. We can actually stay even longer than three months. And off-season it's all empty and cheap – the boats too.'

'Why can't we go tourist class?' Ann asked.

'I'm too old for that. Have you ever done it?'

'No, when I went to Rome, Harvard got me on a charter plane.'

'I've gone across on the *Queen Mary*, tourist. In a six-by-six cabin with four ageing emigrants with cardboard boxes. The steward talking to you like an army sergeant. Lucus a non lucendo, tourist a non touristo. It was awful.'

'I didn't quite get all that,' she said.

'You're not missing a thing.'

Some days went by; and he had the feeling that Ann changed the subject whenever he wanted to discuss it. 'Have you found out at your office whether they'd be willing to let you go?' he asked, and she answered, 'No, not yet, I must wait for the psychological moment.'

'When will you ask?'

'I'll decide on Monday.'

On Monday he avoided prodding her on the telephone, but when he met her at the end of the day, he saw on her face that something had been decided.

'They refused!' he cried.

'No, no, Philip,' she said.

He had finished with his work before she did, and had come to the Foundation in the car.

'Do you mind driving around a bit?' she asked.

'No,' he said, starting the engine again, 'but please don't keep me in suspense. I can see on your face that they've been nasty to you. Those blasted schoolmasters. . . .'

She stopped him with her hand on his arm. 'I didn't ask, Philip.'

'You didn't?' he asked highly surprised.

'I had to talk to you first. And I wasn't certain until today.'

He had a sudden idea of what she was going to say.

'I'm pregnant,' she said with a hesitant smile.

He turned the engine off. 'Oh no, Ann,' he said. Then, because her face seemed to become very sad, he hastily added, 'Dear, don't worry, don't worry please. We'll manage, we'll do something.'

She did not answer.

He started the car once more and drove off; he turned until he was back on Fifth Avenue and went south. He didn't speak until they were on the Park Drive.

'You can't be sure of course,' he said. 'Or did you have a test?'

'No, but I'm sure.'

'Well, do have a test, for the hell of it.'

'All right,' she said listlessly.

'Oh come on, Ann, perk up. It's just one of those things. We'll try everything, put you in a hot bath, give you quinine – you poor girl.'

After a while he said, 'Isn't it the damnedest thing though. Such bad luck.'

When she still didn't answer he asked, 'Or have you been careless?'

'No, Philip.'

He shook his head. 'I always thought that with –' he didn't finish his sentence. Oh blast it, he thought, why did this have to happen now. We mustn't let it spoil Europe for us.

He came out on the West Side and going up Broadway he stopped when they passed a pharmacy. 'Perhaps we should buy some pills and things,' he said, 'I know it usually doesn't work that way but we might as well try.'

She did not get out of the car. 'Are you sure you want to mess around with it?' she said.

'What do you mean? Don't you?'

Then he asked, 'How long is it?'

'Four weeks,' she said.

'Oh – but how can you tell so precisely?'

'Because I know when it happened,' Ann said almost inaudibly. 'It was the night after that party, when you had come to get me –'

'But how – ?' he began.

'Because I do know,' she now said bitterly. 'Because I did it on purpose. Because I was such a sentimental fool that I wanted a child with you that night.'

He stared at her, and then he looked at his feet. The rubber of the brake pedal is all worn off, he thought.

He did not know what to answer her. After a moment's hesitation he drove her home.

95

54

THE following days nothing was said about it. One evening Ann, coming home, tossed a parcel from a pharmacy demonstratively on to the couch, but he didn't ask anything and she did not volunteer any information.

That Friday they were supposed to go to Boston for the week-end; Ann's parents had entreated her to come since they hadn't seen her all summer, and her father had sent them a cheque for the travel expenses.

Philip drove over to the apartment after work and decided to go up and see what she would want to do; he found her sitting on the staircase, outside the apartment, her elbows on her knees and her head resting in her hands, her overnight bag beside her.

She looked up and said, 'I thought you'd ring the bell and I'd have to come down. I packed your things for you.' Her voice was toneless.

'Are you sure you want to go?'

'Oh, I think so. They're counting on it.'

He sat down beside her on the stairs. A neighbour came out of the elevator and gave them a hard look before entering his apartment. Philip stared back at him until the man turned his head.

'Ann, did you do anything?' he asked.

'Oh yes, of course I did,' she said resentfully. 'All the tricks. It didn't help. It never does.'

'Oh.' Then he said, 'Do you think going to a doctor is immoral?'

She suddenly began to smile. 'Some months ago we got a letter at the Foundation. It circulated because everybody thought it was so funny. It was from a girl in Denmark who had a scholarship to study in the U.S., she wrote to thank us and then she said she'd just found out that she was pregnant, and she hadn't decided yet whether she was going to have the baby or have an abortion and accept the scholarship. Very matter-of-fact and above-board – a neatly typed letter – that made it so funny.'

Philip felt better; after all it wasn't such a drama. 'What a wonderfully civilized country,' he said. He put an arm around her shoulders.

'Yes.'

'If we fiddle with death and improve on nature we must fiddle with birth too; we can't disrupt the balance. The earth is already so overcrowded that –'

'Oh Philip, be still,' she burst out, 'you don't have to convince me. I don't think birth control or abortions are immoral; everyone has a right to decide these things for himself. Don't you understand? I'll find a doctor. It's just that I feel bitter about your reaction; you didn't hesitate, not for a second.'

'But we have always said that we didn't want children, not for a long time anyway. You agreed. You should have stuck to the agreement.'

'You're quite right.'

'Well, am I not?'

'I said you were right, didn't I?'

'It didn't sound as if you meant it.'

'That night, when you had left your party and come to mine,' Ann said, 'when we drove home without speaking and sat on the couch here in the dark – and made love – I felt as if we were all new again, as if we had found a new beginning. And suddenly it seemed an unbearable thought that you would come into me and go away again. I loved you so that I wanted something from you to stay with me. That's why I did it.'

He closed his eyes and did not answer.

'And then you started about Europe,' Ann said. 'I knew already that I had made a mistake, that the thought was beautiful but that the reality would be awful – and I thought, it was just once, I won't have the bad luck to be punished so promptly for a mistake. The gods will have mercy on me. But they didn't. Bang, here I am.'

He swallowed. 'I didn't realize,' he said. 'That's a sweet thing to tell me, about wanting to keep something of me – I'm honoured – I don't want the reality to be awful, Ann – let's go ahead with it then.'

'You mean, have a baby?'

'Yes.'

'Are you certain, Philip? Are you sure you can take it? Are you sure you want it?'

He laughed because of her breathlessness. It was a big thing to make her happy, he thought; it was worth it.

'I'm certain,' he said.

Ann kissed him and jumped up. 'I feel as if we should do something,' she said, excited, 'as if we should tell everybody at once.'

'Well, no,' he said reluctantly, getting to his feet.

'I won't, don't worry. But I'm pleased.' She picked up her bag and swung it around.

'Let's go to Boston now,' he said. 'Let's forget the whole business until Monday.'

She studied his face.

'Please don't tell your parents yet,' he asked as he walked down the stairs behind her.

'What about Europe?' she asked over her shoulder.

'Oh, I don't mind that,' he mumbled.

55

PHILIP was very quiet during the week-end with her parents. He was lost in his speculations; he began visualizing their lives. Ann would lose her figure, resign from her job, and then there would be a baby in their apartment. He told himself this was a monstrous reaction and he looked vainly for something appealing or happy about it. It seemed to him the end of all their hopes and plans, of their youth. But men are supposed to feel proud, he thought. But proud of what? Does this show that my love for Ann is insufficient? But if you love a woman how can you shift your love so easily from her to a child? How can you avoid the child coming between you? Well, even literally, he said to himself with a weak smile. Did a woman lose interest or not in love-making after a baby – what had a doctor told him about that once?

But wasn't it true that a curettage was a psychological shock to a woman, even when it was done all legally and decently? Oh what nonsense, he thought, aren't there a million a year in the U.S.? But isn't it still murder? Not at this stage, not now; it is a germ, it doesn't have a soul. Only after six months is it a person – that's the law in California. I always believed in the sacredness of life. Perhaps that is the positive side in this; I must prove myself and stick to that idea, even if it means a screaming child in a one-and-a-half-room apartment – but why did Ann force this dilemma upon us? She had no right to.

There was a growing resentment in him against her or perhaps against the situation.

They weren't alone much that week-end. On Sunday night they drove back to New York in silence. The Massachusetts Turnpike seemed a tunnel without end to him, 'Please go faster,' he asked her, 'I'm going out of my mind.' 'I'm doing seventy,' she told him.

He did not mention Europe any more.

One evening Ann came out with a list of questions about the arrangements they should make. He said, 'Sweetheart, do whatever you want. I'll do my best to behave and help, but I'd rather not be consulted – not at this stage.'

He saw the changing look on her face, and he felt guilty. He wanted to get up and embrace her and say the things he knew she would want him to say. But he was paralysed. 'Dammit,' he muttered, 'I can't always be interrupted. I was trying to work.' And he took his book with him to the bedroom and fell down on the bed with it.

But I must not be this way, he thought. I must not add to the fears and the inhumanity of this world.

56

WHEN he called the Foundation the following morning at eleven he was told Ann had taken the day off. There was no answer from the apartment; she was home when he came in at six. 'I didn't feel well,' was all she said.

The following morning she drove him to Rockefeller Center. 'I need the car,' she said. 'But you'll never be able to park it,' he objected. 'Don't worry about it,' she answered.

She pulled up at the corner of Fifty-first Street and Rockefeller Plaza. 'It's only half past nine,' Philip said, 'Tony will have a fit if I show up at this hour.'

'Have a cup of coffee somewhere,' she said unsmilingly, and drove off with shrieking tires. He stood on the sidewalk and stared after her.

He saw that the light at the corner of Sixth Avenue was turning against her. And then he began to run down the street.

'Ann,' he shouted, 'Ann, wait – you don't understand – I'm sorry I was beastly – Ann, please wait –'

She did not look around; he didn't know whether she heard him or not.

He brushed against passers-by; an acrid taste rose up in his mouth.

He was not more than thirty feet away from her when the light changed and the line started moving. She accelerated hard and drove across the avenue, going west.

He telephoned her several times but she was neither at the Foundation nor at home.

At six he found the car double-parked in front of their house with a green parking ticket dangling from the windshield wiper. His heart began to beat very fast. The elevator wasn't there; he went up the stairs.

Ann was lying in bed, staring at the ceiling.

'Ann,' he said, 'are you all right?'

She turned towards him and looked at him – ironically, he thought, something between pity and irony?

'Did you have a curettage?' he asked.

'Why,' she said, 'didn't you want me to? I'm sorry, in that case you're too late.'

57

ANN stayed in bed for three days and he made a great effort to please her; he bought books and magazines, and frozen dinners, fruit and other things from the delicatessen. He prepared elaborate meals and served them to her on a tray. She looked appreciative whenever he came in with something; she seemed distracted but not sad or angry any more.

On Monday morning in the agency he realized with a shock at half past eleven that she had skipped their call, for the first time; but when he called her and mentioned it she only said that she had been too busy because of the days she had missed. The following days she called him again at eleven. Once or twice during her lunch hour she went to see her own doctor; when he asked her about it, she said that everything was fine. He didn't dare ask more.

One evening after dinner he said, 'Ann, this is nonsense, please tell me all that happened. I want to know, I don't want you to be alone with this.'

She shrugged. 'It doesn't make any difference now. I was alone at the time. I'd rather forget about it.'

He did not pursue the matter. After a while she looked up from her book and volunteered, 'But you might as well know that we'll have to postpone any trips to Europe.'

'Oh?'

'I had to take out a bank loan,' she said. 'I have only one hundred dollars left in my account now, and three hundred to pay off over the next six months.'

'Lord,' he muttered. 'That's a blow. I'll help, Ann, I will indeed. I'll get some free-lance job on the side, I'll work like the devil.'

'Oh no,' she said, 'I wouldn't dream of it. Why should you have to pay for my mistakes?'

58

IT was about a week later when she came to bed again without wearing panties. She turned off the light as she lay next to him; he asked her, 'Ann, does that mean that you are back in the running?'

First he thought that she had not heard or understood his question. But after a long pause she turned towards him and said, 'I'm not to make love for a month. Or, as the man phrased it, no intercourse until my next ... et cetera. It was a very romantic interview. I love those words.'

'Oh, Missie,' he said softly, 'what does it matter? They're just words.'

He pressed her against him; he felt weak with wanting and hoped that she, feeling that, would caress him. She moved away, almost imperceptibly. Then he finally said, 'Oh, please — '

She turned her back towards him. 'You'd better go to sleep,' she said, 'it's late.'

59

AND then he felt overcome with the concept of what had happened. He tried to imagine how a child of Ann's and his would have looked. I have sinned, he thought, it sounds crazy but there you are – I have sinned, not against some materialistic rule of society, but against our idea of search, of being lost and found, of our destiny.

And yet if Ann had not done this, if we had gone through with it, we would have drowned that idea in a pool of domesticity.

I am unable to translate my dream into hard rock daily reality. But I have to learn that. Ann is my reality. I must learn that, and then, perhaps, we will have another child one day. He found some peace in the thought.

He could not bring any of this up with her; the vaguest allusion made her withdraw into a shell.

November settled on the city and with it a fine drizzle which seemed to have no end; at times in the night the wind rose and then the rain would change into a hard slanting curtain of water rattling on roofs and windows. In the morning they would run downstairs with an umbrella and a towel to wipe the seat of the car which always got wet in the night although there were no visible leaks in the top.

He would drive her silently to her office, insisting on her staying in the car until he had manoeuvred it right in front of the door. Then he would struggle down Park Avenue, wiping the steamed-over side window with his handkerchief and peering around for a parking space amidst the jostling, dripping traffic.

60

PHILIP had invited Robert Murray for drinks at the apartment; it would help to distract Ann with other people. Since then Murray dropped in about once a week, and surprisingly he now got on much better with Ann than with Philip who was very reserved. 'I know he's a bastard,' Ann once said in a half-amused tone after Murray had left, 'but at least he's not one atom a hyprocrite.'

The big champagne party given by the president of the General Assembly at the UN came up and Murray invited them; Ann hesitated and said, without consulting Philip, that she didn't think she'd want to go. But on the actual evening of the party, when they were sitting on the couch and reading, she suddenly jumped up and said, 'Oh, let's go.' It took Philip a moment to know what she meant.

The car was parked several blocks away. 'Please get a cab,' she asked, 'I don't want to hike.' She was wearing a yellow and white silk dress which left her shoulders bare. He had never seen her in it before and he couldn't stop staring at her in the taxi; she has such lovely shoulders, he thought. She caught his look.

In the Conference Building of the United Nations a huge crowd was milling around; two bands were playing. He danced with her but rather badly, and when the tune came to an end she walked off the dance floor with him. He saw many people follow her with their eyes. A man came up to them whom he didn't know; Ann introduced him to Philip and then accepted his invitation to dance.

From then on Philip rather lamely trailed behind her; he didn't have the slightest desire to be on his own or dance or talk with another woman. When Ann danced he felt lost and imagined people staring at him, standing alone amongst the small and big groups. He was glad when he caught sight of Tony and button-holed him for a talk about the news agency.

Ann drank champagne all evening, very much of it. An unlimited supply of champagne had always seemed the height of luxury to him but now after two glasses he could not drink another drop. They never saw Murray.

When they were back home, he stood in the dark bedroom with her and whispered, 'Ann, please. Let me, let us make love again.'

'Yes,' she said, and turning her back towards him, 'please unhook my dress.'

She did not want any preliminaries; she was very hard and

104

quick with him. 'Fill me, fill me,' she said hoarsely, angrily almost, beating on his back with her fists.

The following morning she was silent and withdrawn as she had been all the preceding mornings of hasty breakfasts and wet silent car rides to the Foundation.

61

'JOHN IRWIN got married,' she said thoughtfully. They had just come home and were looking through their mail; she was sitting in the chair near the window and he was leaning against the doorway to the kitchen. 'Who told you?' he asked.

'He's sent me an announcement. He's in Chicago now.'

'I hope you're not sorry it isn't you?'

'Don't be foolish,' she answered.

They did a great deal of reading those days; reading and movies filled most of their hours together. They had many arguments but not about personal matters – about politics and books and ideas. Philip could get as involved in an abstract discussion as in a personal one, and when he became impatient or raised his voice Ann immediately drew back and said she didn't care that much. 'I'm very bored with my job,' she told him. 'I wish I could do something creative. I'll never get any farther in that dreary Foundation. Any twenty-year-old boy fresh out of college has more possibilities after one week with us than I after four years. Women are second-rate citizens.' Philip had heard her speak in such terms before; he used to hold forth on the glories of being a woman and how one could not love a woman who did not love herself; he was silent now.

He had not written the hundred-dollar report for NBC in the turmoil; he was working on other subjects which they had agreed to have him do although on speculation only. That meant he would not get paid for whatever they did not use.

They had re-established a routine, and part of it was that

they made love again – before going to sleep. Nothing was different technically; but now they never spoke about it any more. An intensity of feeling which seemed within their grasp again while he was holding her, eluded them at the last moment. He stayed in the shadow of the frustration he had felt after Ann's curettage; he found himself thinking of women, women in novels and movies, and the real women walking around the skating rink of Rockefeller Center at lunch-time.

It was still true, he thought, that only Ann, only the idea of her womanhood, was exciting to him.

But the reality of all others was there, he had rediscovered them; he was aware again of the loveliness of the world on which so many beautiful women lived, and he could not return to his mental monogamy. He wanted to; for that state of mind was now linked with Ann's and his beginnings, with the 'end of the search', their golden age, about which he thought with a nostalgia that slowly became more and more melancholy.

62

AT one of Laura's evenings Philip found himself sitting next to a hard and eager-looking girl who started talking with him about travelling and about Europe. They found themselves in disagreement about every subject that came up and insulted each other in a mild way. In the middle of a sentence of his the girl stood up and went out to get her coat; he walked with her. He helped her into it and she asked, 'Will you take me home?'

'I'm sorry, I can't,' he said after a moment. 'I'm not alone here.'

'Oh,' she said. 'My name is Audrey – Audrey Holding. Do you want to come later?'

He put his hands on her shoulders and felt the rough wool of her coat, then he kissed her on her mouth. She kissed him back with great concentration. He shook his head, at himself rather, and slowly went back to the other room without looking around.

He was perturbed and guilty. His first thought was to see where Ann was and whether she had been watching him. It took him some time to discover her in a small group talking heatedly about jazz.

He got himself a drink and sat on a couch near-by; when Ann saw him she came over and fell down next to him on the couch. She took the glass out of his hand and had a long sip. 'Oh, I'm so thirsty,' she said, 'and exhausted. We've tried to dance to all sorts of crazy music.'

This made him feel better about his behaviour with Audrey Holding. He thought, parties are to be irresponsible, everybody is doing it.

'Let's be modern,' he said.

'Oh yes, let's,' Ann agreed, with such definiteness that it gave him a pang of jealousy. 'Just how modern is modern?' he asked her.

'Oh you,' she said. 'You're a hundred women and a hundred parties ahead of me.'

'You're mad,' he protested.

'How many women have you known in your life?' Ann asked. 'I mean "known" in the biblical sense. Tell me. Don't be secretive, I'm not jealous.'

'I don't know. You think I made notches on my rifle?'

'A hundred?'

'Oh no!'

'Well, how many, then?'

'Perhaps ten,' he said embarrassed, not knowing what to answer.

'Only ten?' Ann asked, pouting. 'You disappoint me.'

'Well, twelve then.'

'All right. That means I can have ten men. Then we're even.'

'A splendid idea.'

'Don't you think so?' she asked blithely.

He gave her a startled look. 'Ann, you're not serious!' he cried.

She patted him on his cheek. 'No, of course I'm not serious,' she said.

63

AFTER that evening a mood of restlessness took hold of Ann. They talked about wandering over the world, about what being an adventurer was like, and she came up with the idea that the excitement of newness and of conquering or being conquered could not be equalled by anything else.

'And I would have liked to be a soldier of fortune,' he said, 'or one of those fellows who wandered from court to court and seduced countesses and made and lost fortunes.'

'Like Stewart Granger in *Scaramouche*,' Ann said.

'Exactly.'

'I know now that you're like that,' she said, 'and it's contagious. It means that we are always waiting, waiting for little and big things. Waiting to have a car, to have the job you want, to move to the country. But of course that's not the way to live. I don't want to waste my best years like that. I'd rather be one of your seduced countesses.'

'Oh Anna,' he said, 'it will be better – I'm not basically like that, not any more. I'll find my berth.'

She didn't look satisfied. 'I had such a staid youth, you know. I want to have some fun before it's too late.'

When they came out of the house that evening they discovered that the first snow was falling. The cold was wet and penetrating; Ann shivered. They had planned to see an old French movie in a theatre on Broadway in the Nineties. 'The car is on First Avenue,' Philip told her. 'Let's take the crosstown bus instead,' she said.

They arrived late; the movie had already begun. As they went to their seats, empty popcorn boxes and old newspapers rustled under their feet. It was too light in the theatre for the shabbiness of the place to be hidden. Only a few people were there.

As Philip watched the film he had to fight a growing feeling of rebellion. Suddenly everything seemed hopelessly and irreparably dreary to him. He studied Ann's profile in the uncertain light.

Life is so daily, he thought.

A half-crystallized thought passed through his mind – how he should have married a rich woman, for wealth was the only antidote against the rut.

The house lights went on. A man in the row ahead of them woke up with a loud yawn.

They came out into the poverty of the West Side street, the dirty snow, the huddling people going by, ugly in their undisciplined discomfort.

'Oh let's get away from here, quick,' he asked.

'I have to buy some things for tomorrow,' Ann said. 'It will only take a minute.'

She entered a grocery store on the corner of Broadway.

He followed her. 'What would you like for dinner tomorrow?' she asked him as they were standing at the meat counter; but seeing his face, she said, 'Why don't you wait outside?'

He left the store without a word. When she finally came out he took the bag from her and as they waited for the light, to cross Broadway, he glowered at her and muttered, 'I really don't think one has to buy groceries at midnight – can't you get organized differently?'

'Oh, I beg your pardon,' Ann said, taking the bag out of his hands again. 'Why don't you fire me?'

'We have a car, you know,' he said. 'We spent two hours in the supermarket last Saturday. Can't you buy your stuff for a whole week?'

'I forgot some meats,' Ann began to explain. Then she became angry too. She started to cross although the light was still red; a bus barely missed her and muddied her stockings. 'Why don't you go to a hotel,' she said over her shoulder.

He ran after her and caught up with her at the next corner. He took hold of her arm to make her stop.

She looked at his drawn face in the grey light of the street lamp filtering through the wet flakes which were now falling densely.

'I don't like you, Philip,' she said. 'And you are ugly.'

64

ANN wanted to go to her parents for Thanksgiving and they decided it might be good for both of them if she went alone. They did not quite know whose idea it had been originally but she agreed it would help her nerves; she said she had not felt too well the past weeks. She was going to take a train on Wednesday in the early afternoon straight from her office, and she was not coming back until Monday morning – to avoid the holiday crowds. Philip's feelings were mixed. It came as something of a shock to him that it was tempting to be completely free for five nights. Yet he thought he would be lonely; and to spend Thanksgiving alone was extremely unappealing. He would rather have come along with Ann if it hadn't been for one trivial fact: he discovered that he wanted to look up Audrey Holding.

Miss Holding had not impressed him at all as a woman; she was neither beautiful nor even very interesting. But he could not dismiss the thought that those words of hers 'do you want to come later' had meant that she had wanted him, that she had wanted him after knowing him for one hour, and that she had felt no need to hide that desire. There was something magnetic in this to him.

On Wednesday Ann and Philip had lunch together in a restaurant on Madison Avenue near her office; she started telling him about the food supplies in the house but interrupted herself to say, 'Oh, you're probably thinking I'm crazy – I know you'll be all over the place; you won't want to eat at home of course.'

Philip made a doubtful face.

'If you have time, go look up the Greggs,' Ann said. He thought about that and said to himself that it wouldn't do; they would think it very odd for him to be in New York alone.

He walked her back to the Foundation, where she picked up

her bag; he hailed a taxi for her on Fifth Avenue. He kissed her good-bye; she turned the window down before giving the driver her destination and put her hand out with a smile. He pressed it and blew her a kiss. A car behind the taxi started to honk, and she drove off, her face turned towards him at the rear window. Then he walked back to the news agency.

He finished with his bulletin at five o'clock; there had been little news coming in. Tony was putting on his coat as he handed in his sheets; he waited for him to leave and then he telephoned Audrey Holding. There was no answer.

He now decided to go for the car first; they had parked it the day before in the Nineties and left it there. He went down and came out of the building at the exit on Fifty-first Street. Crowds were filling the sidewalks; the street was solid with taxis. He thought he wouldn't fight his way into a bus but would walk; that way he'd give Audrey Holding more time to get home too.

65

IT was a long walk up Fifth Avenue and it led him through the holiday evening of the town. First past the decorated stores, then along the hotels north of Fifty-seventh Street; he made his way through groups of people waiting for taxis and looked at couples entering and coming out of the lobbies. There was much loud talk and laughter round him.

Then without transistion the avenue became almost deserted. The light was fading rapidly. A young man and woman passed him; they were in evening clothes and she said, 'We shouldn't be late, dear.' He felt a pang of longing and of regret.

He came to the car at Ninety-third Street and Second Avenue. Here the brilliant twilight of midtown had given way to a cold hard night; he entered a bar and looked up Audrey Holding's number again. The time was 6.25; he decided to call her at half past six. The bar was empty; he bought a Scotch and drank it leaning against the stand with the telephone directories.

When he entered the booth, he thought, I won't call again after this; but after four rings he felt deeply disappointed. Then someone answered after all.

'Hello,' a girl's voice said.

'Hello, Audrey, this is Philip.' He wondered whether she would remember him.

'Audrey isn't here,' the voice said.

'Who is this?' he asked.

'Her room-mate. Audrey's gone home for Thanksgiving.'

'Oh,' Philip said. 'Where's that?'

'In Chatham. That's New Jersey. She'll be back on Sunday.'

'Thanks – sorry to have bothered you.'

'That's all right,' the girl answered. 'Have a nice Thanksgiving.'

He hung up hastily – he felt hot, he was embarrassed at what he had done. Thank God she wasn't there, he thought.

He paid for his drink and drove down Second Avenue to Seventy-ninth Street, but as he reached it he slowed down and hesitated – he didn't want to go up to the empty apartment. He could go to a movie and eat out afterwards. Rather shabby to sit alone in a restaurant on an evening like this.

He started to drive east. Seventy-ninth Street was unusually empty; there was parking space in front of his door. He decided to go home.

He opened some cans and ate while reading; at half past eight he called Ann, person to person, so as not to have to talk to her parents.

It took some time before she came to the telephone.

'Hello, Philip,' she said immediately, 'I knew it was you. Sweet of you to call.' Her voice sounded very much more happy and relaxed than it had in New York.

'Is everything all right?' was all he could thing of asking.

'Oh yes, fine. I had a good trip, not very crowded really. And we're having a beautiful dinner right now – ' she was off the telephone for a moment – 'and my parents and everybody else send their love. They're sorry you couldn't come.'

'Well, give them my greetings,' he said.

112

'I will. Take care of yourself now. And eat.'

'Bye Ann,' he said, and then, hastily, 'Ann – happy Wednesday.'

There was a silence at the other end in which he could hear the buzz of voices in the background.

'Happy Wednesday, Philip,' she then answered.

66

THE following morning Philip woke up and saw to his dismay that it was only eight o'clock. He drew the curtains and went back to bed; he lay there staring at the ceiling. The day ahead of him seemed endless; without Ann I don't have anything in New York, he thought. I must build up more of a life here.

A click of the alarm clock startled him. 'Ten minutes to nine,' he said aloud. He turned and looked at the clock until the small hand had uncovered the hand of the alarm. Ten to nine, it says, he thought; day and night the hand of the alarm shows that we get up at ten to nine. I want to be freed from the trivia of life.

Suddenly he saw himself sitting on a bench, on the deck of a ship. An old piano was standing on the deck; a net was hanging in front of it. Why the net? he asked himself, but then he saw that two boys were playing ping-pong behind the piano. The net was to prevent the ball from getting lost. A tall man sat down behind the piano and started playing the St Louis Blues. The ship's public-address system carried the music, quite loudly. Knuckles O'Toole, Philip thought. But then it can't be that man playing – it must be a record. I am dreaming.

He shook himself and woke up. For a moment he felt a deep fear travel through him. He could still hear the music, bare-boned music, he thought. Nothingness, awaiting me.

He hastily went to the bathroom, shaved and dressed, and left the house.

It was very quiet on the street. He started the car and drove down Lexington Avenue until he came to a drug-store which was open. He ordered coffee and eggs; the counter man brought the coffee first, a thick cup, overflowing into the saucer. Philip got off his stool and bought some stationery; the clerk lent him his ball-point. As he ate his breakfast he wrote a letter to Ann; and as soon as he started writing he felt better.

He told her that he missed her and hoped she was having a good time; she should take it easy and let her parents wait on her all they wanted because she needed some rest and luxury. 'I'm sorry for many things,' he wrote. 'I'll try and do better when you get back.'

'Anything else?' the counter man asked as Philip was licking the envelope and closing the letter. Philip smiled at him and shook his head.

He drove down to the Grand Central post office and sent his letter special delivery. As he came out again, the four days ahead of him had lost their frightening endlessness. He started the car and turned on the radio.

67

PHILIP went to the Greggs' after all and had his Thanksgiving dinner with them. Unexpectedly they did not ask for any explanation of Ann's having gone to Boston alone. Everyone is so taken up with his own problems, he thought, and assumes that other people are watching and speculating on them. John has enough to worry about in his own life. They were so eager to have me here, it was more than hospitality; obviously they had been afraid of being alone on this day. What a miserable thought. I wonder what the odds are against a successful marriage – and successful not meaning: keeping up appearances.

Philip stayed in most of the following days and worked on his radio scripts. But he kept thinking about marriage; he read a play and came upon a passage in which a man said, 'You have lost one and gained all the others. . . . You leave the red eyes of your great love and hear the first laughter of a girl on the street.' He was stung by these words; why did I chance to read this now, he thought; it is really like that? Is there happiness only in movement?

He jumped up and searched among his papers until he found Ann's letter about tenderness being a bridge between tension and fulfilment and read it again. But the cards are so heavily stacked against us, he thought. Aren't the great loves in history all tragic ones? If we had hit a tree driving back from Greenwich, or if we had drowned in our Canadian lake after making love on that sand bar – would that have been the true glory? But that's defeatistic, I don't want such a weak and nostalgic idea of love.

On Sunday morning he woke late; and the moment he opened his eyes he planned to call Audrey Holding and try to see her. He dismissed the idea; it would be an unsavoury thing to do, he told himself. And then he thought. What does it matter? Since I know it doesn't mean anything, and since Ann will never know? As long as I don't hurt anyone, why not be a bit hedonistic? Now his only remaining worry was the chance that he'd make a fool of himself, that Miss Holding had forgotten all about him.

At noon he was reading the Sunday paper with a feeling of anticipation because he was going to call her; he stood up to look at himself in the mirror and thought, An adventure, any adventure, is quite different from all other emotions.

Then the telephone rang. He had been so concentrated on his call that he thought it must be Audrey Holding calling him.

He heard the voice of the long-distance operator, Ann spoke, and he was happy that he had not called Audrey yet, that he could talk to Ann before having done such a thing.

'Hello Ann,' he said, 'I'm missing you so.' That was true.

She laughed. 'I'm at South Station,' she said. 'I'm taking the train back, in five minutes. I didn't want to stay away any longer either.'

For a moment he had to fight a sensation of disappointment.

He said, 'I'll be at the station here to get you, Anna. At the information booth. And I'm so glad you're coming back today.'

68

HE drove down fast to Grand Central Station, feeling very free – maybe this is life at its happiest, he thought, to be alone and free and not lonely because the end of your loneliness is in sight. I must tell Ann. Or would she take it amiss? The language is so precise: you can't care and be carefree. Unless it's the wild, all-embracing optimistic caring when you are very young and uncynical. I have almost an hour, I'll have a drink. Let's be expansive. He left the car in front of the Commodore Hotel and gave the doorman the keys; then he went to the bar.

He got to the station with five minutes to spare, but the train was late and he sat on a bench in the vast hall and looked at the people. It wasn't very crowded yet, but the waiting for the masses which would soon start streaming back into the city seemed to fill the air with uneasiness.

'Philip!' he suddenly heard beside him and he turned with a shock. Ann was standing there, slightly out of breath, carrying her suitcase and an enormous bag.

'Well, you might give me a hand, you know,' she said.

He jumped up.

'I kept calling and waving and whistling,' she told him, 'and you went on staring right through me. Most uncanny. You don't seem too delighted to see me.'

He took her things. 'Oh sweetheart,' he said, 'I didn't see you at all, I was just staring into space.'

Ann stood still and smiled again. 'Don't I get a kiss?' she asked.

Someone jostled Philip and he almost dropped the bag. 'Not here,' he said. Ann's smile vanished. Oh damn, he thought, why did I say that. Now it's already spoiled. We should start

116

again, have her get off the train again – she's really too sensitive.

Or does she read something in my face I'm not aware of myself? he wondered as they came out into the street. Their car was still in front of the hotel; he tipped the doorman and they got in.

'Well, that was painless,' Ann said. 'How have you been?'

'Fine. I mean miserable.'

'Are you glad to see me?'

'Yes, of course, Anna.'

They drove on in silence.

'What's in the bag?' he asked.

'All sorts of tricks and treats,' Ann said, cheerful again. 'Presents from my parents. They were sweet.'

'Nothing for me?'

'No – we went shopping yesterday, you know. If you'd been there they would certainly have bought you something.'

'Oh.'

Anna laughed. 'Don't be a child. There's a piece of pumpkin pie there for you.'

The sky had suddenly cleared and the sun appeared, low over the houses and like a dull-red ball. She pointed at it and he nodded.

'Ann,' he asked, 'do you think we're bad for each other's ego?'

'Do you mean that you felt relieved when I wasn't here?'

'No!' he cried. 'But you look happier and better for having been away. Other people always have that effect on you, I've noticed it before. When you're miserable a long speech from me is less comfort to you than the smile of a bus driver.'

'You look better too,' Ann said.

'A disconcerting comment on marriage.'

'I did think one thing while I was away,' she said. 'It's too much my show here. Perhaps that's bad. It's my town and my friends and my furniture. We might have done better in California.'

'Would you come with me to California?'

'I expect so. If it were very important for you to go. Of course I'd go with you.'

117

'Do you think you'd like it there?' he asked.

'No,' Ann said with an unexpected definiteness that made them both laugh.

'Murray told me about a place called Parkway Village,' she said. 'On Long Island. Built for the United Nations people but open to everybody now.'

'That sounds like one of those ghastly developments.'

'I know, but he said it wasn't like that at all. Solid houses and all very green.'

'Yes, perhaps we should get out of Manhattan after all,' he answered. 'Let's go have a look at it some day.'

'Yes. In early spring perhaps.'

When Ann unpacked, he saw her take his special-delivery letter out of her suitcase. She had kept it in a book and she now put it away very carefully with other letters in her drawer.

She looked up and he hastily turned his head and pretended not to have noticed. He felt a sudden, burning, compassion for her which brought tears to his eyes. That letter was better than I am, he thought.

I do not live up to her dream.

69

THERE were times when Philip woke up in the night in panic. Then he lay still in the dark room and tried to catch the sound of Ann's breathing; it was a light, reassuring sound. After a while he couldn't distinguish it any more from the pounding of the blood in his ears.

He told himself that he was a coward and a weakling but that did not help. It was the fear of death which had taken hold of him. The universe will go on for ever and ever, he thought, and without us. At such moments it seemed almost inconceivable to him that mankind could continue living in the shadow of that certainty. We've built all sorts of false securities around us. Counting the years. What does it mean, 'the year 1960'? It screens off a piece from eternity, but not really; it is like a cabin with only two walls, on an endless lot.

The oceans brake the movement of the turning earth and each hundred years a second is thus added to the length of a day. And the years go faster as we are nearing the sun; there is no measure of man in the universe. Our sacred order of things is only a flash in an endless change. Come on, come on, he would mutter, let's get on with the order of the day. Think of war, think of charging a machine-gun with certain death in front of you. He would whisper the Lord's Prayer.

Then it would pass. We're all in the same boat, he would say to himself.

He moved, until he could feel the warmth of Ann's body. He was grateful for her presence.

But if we have only one life, he thought, shouldn't we live it very, very much? Aren't the hedonists right? Or the existentialists, or the tricheurs, or whatever they are – the people who want to squeeze life, catch every drop? How else can man survive mortality? Just live – the world is so big. And for the first time it's all there, it's all available. Every land, every town, every woman – if you really want it. What a lovely idea.

Anatomy is my only cure – that's what that man in the Dostoevski book meant, that the only cure for life is a woman's body. But what should one do then to live beyond the ending of the search for one's woman? How can one survive the fulfilment of one's love?

He didn't try to talk about this to Ann and he didn't tell her about his night fear. He did say to himself sometimes the phrase which had stuck in his mind: Anatomy is my only cure.

70

ONE day Ann drove him to Parkway Village, the United Nations housing project. They liked it and she went to the agent's office where she tentatively reserved a garden apartment for the first of March. 'Can we put the idea in the ice-box,' he asked as they were back on the parkway to Manhattan, 'just for a week or so? I don't feel quite up to it right now.'

'We don't have to do it at all,' Ann said. 'I thought of it in the first place because it might cheer you up. You hate Manhattan so.'

'Oh, hate – ' Philip said. 'I think it's nice, this Parkway Village, I mean. I'd just like not to think about it right now.'

'Well, in any case, I'm going to make the most of my winter in Manhattan,' Ann announced.

She began lavishly to mail in cheques for plays about to open, and went to exhibitions and ate out as much as possible; since she had taken the bank loan she had completely lost interest in saving money. 'I used to be very much in the swim,' she said. 'I'm sorry I lost track so; why live in New York otherwise?'

Philip was not a very satisfactory escort. Although he did not have too clear an idea of what had happened in art or literature since he had left Berkeley, he felt above it all and listened to earnest conversations on these subjects with an indulgent smile which was rather irritating to Ann. If it fitted in with her day she went to exhibition openings at lunch-time or after work, without him; and she joined theatre parties of friends. 'You're invited of course,' she'd tell Philip – and he would answer in a mixture of pride and listlessness, 'No, thanks, you go with them.' Then he would change into jeans and an old sweater and slouch in a chair with his book; the moment she had closed the door behind her, he'd be annoyed with himself for being such a fool.

Alone in the apartment, he became terribly restless. If Ann went to the theatre without him, she always came straight home afterward and she would tell him about the play with enthusiasm or disgust. 'I hope you got some work done,' she would say, because he was doing texts for NBC and she would usually find him at the desk with papers all around him. 'Yes,' he would assure her, even if he had spent the best part of his time alone in a neighbourhood movie house.

Once, alone in the house, he called Audrey Holding, on the spur of the moment. She did remember him and sounded quite pleased to hear from him.

'I thought you had forgotten all about me,' she said.

'Oh, heavens no,' Philip said. 'No man could.'

'Then why didn't you call before?'

'I have been very busy.'

'Oh yes, I can imagine with what,' she said coyly.

Philip managed a wicked laugh. 'I'm being sophisticated,' he said. 'Temptation should not be too quickly yielded to.'

'Do I tempt you?' she asked.

'You'll find out one day.'

'When?'

'When I'm back from California,' he improvised. 'I'll be away from New York for some time.'

'Oh, it's just a silly game,' he said aloud to the silently watching room after he had hung up.

71

ONE evening they were reading in bed; Ann put her book aside and turned over. 'You can go on reading if you want to,' she said. 'The light doesn't bother me.'

'Sure?'

'Sure.'

After a moment she added in a drowsy voice, 'Wake me up if you want to make love to me.'

He kept looking at his page while thinking about what she

had said. He ended by dropping the book on the floor and turning off the light. Then he moved closer to her and kissed her back.

He had not wanted to commit himself, but she took his hand and pressed it against her body, and he caressed her. Shall I come to her, he asked himself. And just then Ann, feeling the lack of warmth in his caress, pushed his hand away.

He gave her a light kiss and lay on his back. He felt sleep coming over him when Ann suddenly said in a wide-awake voice, 'Philip?'

'Yes?'

'It's rather awful, isn't it?'

'What is?' he asked though he guessed what she meant.

'Our love-making. We can take it or leave it now.'

He was hurt by the 'we' in her sentence.

72

HE took her to dinner in the Village; she chose the restaurant. The owner welcomed her warmly and made them look at an exhibition of drawings in the back room. Several guests greeted her and the painter whose drawings were on show sat down at their table and talked to her for a while. Philip was very polite to them all, but he was watching as an outsider; I wish Ann were harder, he thought, less serious, less artisty. It would be more fun, everything would be simpler, if she — if she would swing a bit.

'What do you think of him?' Ann asked Philip just then as the painter walked away.

'He doesn't swing,' he answered.

She gave him a surprised look.

The service was very slow and Philip finally went to the proprietor and said, 'We're going to the theatre — please hurry a bit. We have been sitting here for an hour.'

'I hope you weren't unpleasant,' she said when he came back to the table.

Philip shrugged. 'He's just a fellow running a crummy restaurant, Ann. He charges enough. We need less arts and crafts here and more service.'

They had to leave their coffees unfinished and walked as fast as they could to the theatre which was only a few blocks away. Philip had never been there and had expected something amateurish, full of good intentions; he was unprepared for the shock of what seemed to him great drama. He looked at Ann who was watching the play with a half-smile on her face, a proprietary smile, he thought, as if this were her creation – she is the ideal audience.

His ideas from earlier that evening now made a complete turnabout. But this is reality, he said to himself, this is what life is about; she has the courage to look for it, the courage to be human. The in-people, the Murrays, they swing, they are all very pleasant and very unobnoxious, but they are just decoration on the earth.

In the intermission they stepped out into an alley running along the theatre, for it was very hot in the audience.

Ann looked at him and he said, 'Oh yes, it is terrific, and terrifying.'

'Thank God you're with it,' she answered, 'I'd have screamed.'

She turned her face towards the ribbon of whitish light sky between the buildings.

'Oh,' she sighed, it sounded like a groan. 'Oh, it's so beautiful – it makes me want I don't know what. It makes me want to be a man.'

She stood with clenched fists and very bright eyes; he thought, I'll never forget how she looks just now.

He said to her, 'But you're such a divine woman.'

73

THE outer world took hold of them again and they went from day to day, not certain of what exactly they were waiting for.

Spring, he thought, we will move, and see trees and grass. There was a connexion between the fading emotions and the city's high blind walls, its noise and dust, its glaring heat and cold, the staring into the rows of anonymous eyes in the buses and the subways, the car horns crying at each other, 'Me!' 'Me!' 'Me!' 'Me!' The giant clip joint.

It is degrading, he thought, and not human. So many hours, so many days, living like ghosts, the rent, and the supermarket. Just to stay alive.

My old desert island, dusted off again. And why not? I won't give up, I won't give in.

74

A COPY of the *Times* was sticking out of his wastepaper basket at the agency. It was folded at the society page and as he was sitting in front of his typewriter he stared at the faces of fiancees and brides peering over the edge.

With an effort he returned to an item on plans for an aluminium factory in South-east Asia. When he had finished with it, he focused on one portrait in the paper, a girl of an English-type beauty, her very young and haughty face untouched by any doubt. He tried to read her name but all he could see was . . . l Phyfe. That was the name of the photographer.

I don't want to know her name, he thought. But then he couldn't resist the curiosity to find out whether she was there because she had got married, or engaged, or whatever. He fished the paper out without getting up from his chair; he almost crashed backward against the radiator. She was Miss Pamela Warren, seventeen; 'Well, Miss Warren,' he said to her, 'sight unseen I already almost broke my skull in your honour.'

Miss Warren was in the paper as a débutante; she was the daughter of Mrs Witts, and Mr and Mrs M. Morgan Witts were giving a dinner dance for her at the Starlight Roof. Mr Warren was unmentioned; how had he faded so silently out of the picture, by a timely death or an unfortunate second marriage? Pamela Warren, he thought, very rich, very cold, deep down a spark which would start a big fire; how possible it would be for a man to conquer her. What a strange life there was to be lived with such a girl, on those heights of the really rich, in their amoral disciplined perpetual self-indulgence.

Or perhaps it wouldn't be that way at all; perhaps Pamela Warren would soon enough be beset by some bodily problem, hepatitis, or psychiatry, or the taxes, or the recognition of Red China. But now she looked still way beyond and above all that, as far away from it as a marble statue. I would like to breathe in that air – just a whiff.

'Any problem, Philip?' Tony shouted, clearly wondering about the long silence of his typewriter so shortly before closing time.

'Oh go to hell,' Philip muttered and shouted back. 'No, I've got it under control.'

There is nothing like youth, he thought. In the end Pamela Warren is closer to almost any other girl of seventeen than to her mother Mrs Witts who is working on the guest list for the Starlight Roof. Starlight a non star lucendo.

Tony looked over the partition and said, 'What on earth are you doing? Do you know it is half past five?'

'Tony,' he answered, 'how old do you think I am?'

'Twenty-six on our personnel list. Mentally, I wouldn't dare guess. Did you get that aluminium factory?'

'Oh yes. Isn't it an awful bore? We both know they'll never build the damned thing.'

75

On New Year's eve they decided to stay at home; they drank Scotch and for twelve o'clock they had a bottle of champagne, sent over by Murray before his return to Los Angeles. Next year we'll be in a house, in Parkway Village, Philip thought.

But he did not do anything about it and Ann didn't mention the project any more either. He was content to leave it up in the air; and to move there began gradually to seem like an investment he was afraid to make.

For now his desert island began to lose its hold on his mind. He began to admit to himself that he was 'not happy' – those words were the only formula in which he allowed his vague cluster of ideas about the search as the only cure for death to be phrased. He nursed the thought that all they needed was some kind of mutual freedom; he did not want this freedom for any concrete purpose, but he wanted them both to proclaim it.

He started debates with Ann on love, conquests, adventures, one person having a monopoly on another. 'We live in a break of the times regarding marriage,' he said.

He quoted her words back at her that the excitement of being conquered, of the first moment, could not be matched by anything else. Ann shrugged and said that that had been a passing mood with her, that everyone had spells of belated adolescence.

'Oh Ann,' he said, 'that's not all it is. Please don't think that. You believed in the knighthood idea –'

She smiled. 'Perhaps adolescents are the only honest people on earth,' she said. And when she sometimes took up his freedom idea or carried it even further, he felt greatly relieved and as if, now that it had been formulated, he should be as warm as possible to her, should woo her anew.

She also had a different reaction. 'If you have an itching foot, go man, go,' she once said.

126

'Would you be there when I got back?'

She was not amused. 'I don't know. Perhaps, if no one more interesting entered on the scene in the meantime.'

'I could never be interested in another woman,' he hastened to tell her.

'You don't have to say that.'

The night in the snow, on Broadway, she had told him to go to a hotel; he had known that she meant it and she had confirmed that later.

At such a moment he thought, Well, here it is, the door reopened. But then immediately a chill went through his body.

He made himself think of one of the many things she had said or done and he was overcome by a surge of tenderness towards her. He thought of her looking at him with her eyes half-closed at their shell-breaking ceremony in the park, of the two children in her ex-libris, of her hurt face when she was standing alone near the bookshelf at Laura's first party; of the way she walked, of her fears and her courages, of her tears, of the souvenirs, the letters, the champagne cork, which she kept in a box in her drawer, and he thought he could never be away from her.

76

HE thought of an evening in Los Angeles. He was driving along Sunset Boulevard in the dusk; below him the lights of the city were patterned in a painfully blue sky. The car radio played loud music, 'Jonah Jones,' the announcer said. He rested his left arm against the outside of the car door; a car pulled up next to him at the traffic light, there was a girl behind the wheel. 'Hey there – ' he sang to her, and drove off on the changing light without daring to look and see her reaction. He grinned at himself.

He had a sudden feeling as if his heart would burst; there is nothing more than this, he thought, nothing can be more than twilight, and jazz, the wind from driving an open car, the tight endless sky; all that combined is the real American dream, the American nostalgia, worth all the wrongs –

And to be young, he now thought, it has to happen to you when you are eighteen.

I let the chance go by.

Something has eluded me and now it is too late, for all time.

'Hollywood has lovely green hills,' he said to Ann. 'Except for all the bill-boards, and the developments they're bulldozing out of them, and the trash along the roadsides.'

She half-smiled at him.

'I used to read the Psalms,' he said. 'This is about the only thing in the Bible I know by heart: "I will lift up mine eyes unto the hills from whence cometh my help."'

'I like that,' Ann answered, puzzled.

77

ANN became very restless when she had to stay in evenings; they had had few party invitations during the Christmas season and she felt hurt by this and blamed his anti-social behaviour for it. Philip knew she was right but he had great difficulty in making himself go out to her kind of parties and talk about the things of the day. He was restless too, but his restlessness was deeper.

Early in January Ann told him that the painter they had met in the restaurant had invited them to a big house-warming. She did not ask his opinion and Philip only answered, 'Oh yes? Where is he going to live?'

'West Twenty-second Street – a huge loft.'

'Have you seen it?'

'Yes, he showed it to us once after an opening.'

Philip felt that he was included in the invitation only because the man could not ask Ann alone; something in her manner of telling him had made that clear. He resented this; he had certainly tried to be polite in the restaurant. He thought that Ann should not have been in on this at the other side of the fence, as he called it for himself, and he decided that he would on no account go.

When he came home on the evening of the party Ann, who had gone ahead by bus, said, 'I hope you don't mind a quick dinner out of cans. I want to take a bath, and dress, and we shouldn't be there much after eight.'

'I didn't know we were going,' he answered.

'Oh Philip,' Ann cried indignantly, 'I told you a week ago.'

'You just mentioned it. You didn't ask me whether I wanted to go. I'd rather not.'

Ann sat down by the window and looked silently out into the street.

After a while she said, 'It's not fair. You should have told me if you didn't want to go.'

He answered, 'Please go all the same. You'll have much more fun. I don't belong with that crowd at all.'

'What crowd – there is no crowd,' Ann retorted. She got up and went into the kitchen.

They ate dinner without speaking much, and then she put on a housecoat and started washing the dishes.

He came to the kitchen and stood behind her, putting his hands on her shoulders. She tried to turn away but he held on and said, 'Come on, sweetheart, you go to your party. We said we'd be modern and all that. I really don't want to see those people.'

She turned around and looked thoughtfully at him. 'All right,' she said slowly.

She dropped her dishcloth and vanished into the bathroom. He heard her showering hastily and then she dashed into the bedroom, 'It's past nine o'clock,' she complained.

'It'll still be on.'

Ann came out into the living-room in her yellow-and-white silk dress, carrying her shoes. 'I had no time to do my nails,' she said almost apologetically, 'but one finger I just had to fix.'

He was huddled in a chair with the paper and he did not react. He looked at her as she waved her left hand to dry the nail polish and put the car keys and her compact into an evening bag. She stepped into her shoes; there was something frantic about her preparations that was disturbing.

She was already opening the front door when he got up and came towards her. 'Please be careful,' he said.

She gave him an impatient glance. 'Why do you look that way,' she said, 'I thought you wanted to be modern.'

'Of course.'

'Don't wait up for me. But I'm sure I'll be back by eleven.'

78

PHILIP went to the kitchen after she had gone and finished the cleaning up there; he left the light in the living-room on and went to bed.

He woke up, after what he thought was a short time, from the sound of her steps. I must be very nice to her, he decided; I've been rather unpleasant.

The steps passed the door of the apartment and died away. How strange, he thought confusedly, steps are either somebody's or they aren't – they can't be *almost* her steps, it's her or it is not at all and wholly not her.

He put the lamp on and looked at the clock. It was two in the morning. Suddenly his throat felt dry and his heart started beating fast. What has happened, he thought. Oh – it's just a party. It might go on till all hours. He turned off the light and lay still in the dark.

When he turned the light on again it was only twenty minutes later. On an impluse he jumped out of bed and called Information. There was no listing in the name of the painter. He stood hesitantly in the dark bedroom. I can't sleep, he said to himself, I might as well get dressed.

He felt relieved with that decision; he had a premonition he would meet her at the elevator and he thought she'd feel sorry she had made him get out of bed.

He was rather indignant now and he dressed hurriedly to be out before her return. But he met her neither at the elevator nor in the lobby.

The street was deserted. He walked to one corner and then to another; she'd come up First Avenue, he thought, but he couldn't be certain. He went back to the house; the elevator had gone. Perhaps I just missed her, he said to himself; he went up but the apartment was as he had left it. He entered the bedroom. It was past three now. Oh, to hell with it, he thought, I don't even want to know when she comes home. He hastily undressed, turned off all the lights and went back to bed.

He woke up again, knowing he was still alone in the bed, and swore softly. 'What the hell is going on,' he muttered. He stretched out his hand to turn on the light and just then there was the sound of her key in the lock. Thank God, he thought, turning over and pretending to be asleep.

He heard her undress in the living-room; she got into bed very softly, then she whispered, 'Are you asleep?'

'No,' he said. And then indignantly, 'I was terribly worried, where the hell have you been?'

She laughed. 'To three parties,' she answered, 'we went from one to the other. It was terrific.'

'Oh,' he murmured. 'You said you'd be home at eleven o'clock and it's five now. You must be mad.'

He thought he was exaggerating when he said that it was five o'clock, but Ann didn't contradict him. 'Don't be a bore; you could have come,' she said. 'Kiss me.'

He moved towards her and she put her hands behind his head and kissed him very wildly with her mouth open. He suddenly realized that she was terribly excited, so much so that for a moment it numbed him. But then he caught her mood and he caressed her and kissed her as she made him. She moaned and said. 'Please, please come to me now,' and he made love to her and lay beside her; she was trembling. They made love again and it was light when they fell asleep.

It was hard getting up; Ann managed first and she made

black coffee for them. He helped her straighten up things; as he hung her dress for her in the closet he saw that the little loop at the back had become unstitched at one end.

79

AT some moment during the day Philip suddenly began to think of the torn loop.

To his own surprise he found that he could not dismiss it from his thoughts. She must have torn it when she undressed in the dark at home, he said to himself. But the idea that it might have happened at the party, that someone else had done it, gave him a strange pain to which he kept returning. Finally he gave in to it and while he worked, fantasies about this kept flitting through his mind.

When he saw Ann again at lunch-time, the very idea seemed so unreal that he could at last let go of it. And then, while they were drinking their coffee, he heard himself ask, 'Did you take your dress off at one of those three terriffic parties?'

Ann stared aghast at him and cried, 'Are you mad?' and at the same time she turned crimson.

He did not say anything more; they got up, he paid, and he walked her back in silence to her office.

When she called him at five, he did not answer the telephone; and he walked home from the agency looking in shops and book stores on the way and stopping at a bar for a drink. It was past seven when he came in; Ann welcomed him with a smile and, without asking anything, announced, 'Dinner is ready.'

He sat down, she brought their plates. He stared at her; he put his fork down and said, 'I don't feel like eating.'

Ann sat still, looking very upset, then she silently went to the bedroom and closed the door behind her. He listened; she was crying but he didn't go to her. He picked up his fork, threw it down again as loudly as he could, and then stood at the window and stared out into the street. To hell with her, he thought. In the end he decided to eat his dinner.

After a long time Ann left the bedroom, her head averted, and went into the bathroom where he heard her dab her face. She came out and knelt beside him and said, 'Why didn't you come to me?'

He did not answer.

'I don't know whom you talked to . . .' she finally stammered.

He jumped up so suddenly that the chair hit her. 'Nobody talked to me,' he said furiously. 'I'm not on speaking terms with any of those people. I saw your dress. The loop was torn off. That's what caused that mad question. And obviously it wasn't so mad.'

Ann stared at him, then went into the bedroom and came back with the dress. 'You mean this loop here?' she asked.

'Yes, that's what I mean.'

'But it has been like that for a week. I meant to fix it all the time and never did.'

He let the anger rise in him. 'You're a damned liar,' he snapped at her and walked out of the apartment.

80

NOTHING more was said about this for several days and they returned to the normal round of things, but they spoke little to each other. Then one evening Ann came to sit next to him on the couch and said in a low voice, 'Philip, do you remember your question about that party?'

'Yes, what about it?' he said, keeping his voice under control with an effort.

'You have a very uncanny intuition about things,' Ann said, smiling at him. He did not smile back but he managed to keep his face calm. 'Go on,' he said.

'Something did happen. Nothing really; and I wasn't going to tell you. But I can't bear the thought that I lied to you. I feel that would come in between us, and become a wall – the idea frightens me.'

He did not answer.

'Don't you think so?' she asked.

'Yes, I do. It's better to tell,' he said with difficulty.

She waited a moment. Come on, come on, he thought.

'Someone did tear that loop on my dress,' she finally brought out.

'Oh – who?'

'Does that matter?'

He shrugged.

She took a deep breath. 'Oh well,' she said. 'Carl the painter.' She waited again, and when he did not say anything or look at her, she swallowed and went on. 'It was at the end, we had gone back to the loft and I guess we were sort of high ...'

'Who are we – just the two of you?' he interrupted tonelessly.

'No, no – there were two other couples.' She swallowed again. 'I am sorry, dearest,' she then said.

'Go on.'

'Nothing, someone turned the light off, and he kissed me, and ...' She stopped.

'And you made love.'

She jumped up. 'On no, we didn't. Please don't think that.'

'Well, what did you do, then?' he asked angrily.

'Nothing, he tried – we sort of necked, that's when my dress got torn. I didn't want to go on, I said so and he stopped, and then I went home.'

'Do you believe me?' she asked in an anxious voice.

'Oh sure. Tell me, did he kiss you on your mouth?'

'No – yes.'

'Anywhere else?'

'Oh please, Philip, don't torture yourself. I swear nothing real happened.'

'Well, did he?' he shouted.

'On my shoulder, I guess. Oh, please stop.'

'Jesus, you started this. Don't you enjoy discussing it? Doesn't it give you a fresh thrill?'

He thought she was going to storm out of the room but she did not. 'I only told you because I didn't ever want to have lied to you,' she said. 'You said . . .'

'Oh fiddle,' he interrupted, 'of course you shouldn't have told me. But do you think I was going to stop you? Would you have felt this way about lies coming between us if I hadn't found out in the first place? How disgusting it all is. How can you!'

'Please Philip. I was just very high. I'm not interested in that man.'

'Then why did you –'

'He was very sweet to me all evening. And when we walked back to his place I suddenly found myself telling him everything, about us, about our love, and how things had declined, and the abortion . . .' Her voice trailed off. There were tears in her eyes. 'I needed someone to talk to,' she said.

He sighed. 'Oh damn it all,' he said wearily.

'Listen,' he asked her, 'would you do me one big favour and throw away that dress?'

She looked startled. 'Philip, it's just a piece of silk. I've only worn it a couple of times.'

'Do I have to wait until it has been torn off you a couple of times?' he cried.

She went to the bedroom and came out with the dress which she put in his lap. Then she left the room again.

He sat there for a while, staring at it; then he rumpled it into a ball, went to the window and threw it out.

81

PHILIP decided not to forgive her, although he was not quite aware himself of the fact that he had a choice in the matter.

He believed what Ann had told him; at times he suddenly stopped and said to himself, Don't be a sucker, of course she made love to that man. But then he immediately knew again it wasn't so. He had great difficulty dismissing the image of the painter kissing her shoulder, and he was furious with her for telling him. He didn't give her any credit for her motive in doing so, he felt that this was one thing two people could never share. He made very much love to her, in a frenzied and almost inimical way; unspoken was somehow the assertion that if she didn't refuse to have her shoulder kissed by a painter called Carl there was nothing on earth she could refuse him, Philip.

'Can't you forgive me? Don't you think we are even now?' she asked him.

'Why even?'

'We have wronged each other – not quite intentionally – but we have. I would so much love to start with a clean slate now.'

'You haven't wronged me,' he announced. 'We've said we are modern people and you acted accordingly.'

'Does that mean that you want to do the same?'

'Under the circumstances that question seems highly uncalled for.'

There was silence.

'Where have I wronged you?' Philip then wanted to know.

'The abortion,' Ann said almost inaudibly.

'But we had agreed that we did not want any children, and –'

'I know,' she interrupted him hastily. 'I know I can't blame you. It just seemed such an utter rejection of me, without a moment's doubt. Perhaps if you hadn't said at one point that you did want – oh well, anyway –'

'Listen Ann,' he said sharply, 'I really don't see why it was a rejection of *you*. Anyway, I am very sorry if you feel that I wronged you. But I hope you don't think I'm happy about that mess. But two wrongs, et cetera, et cetera.'

'I thought you said I had not wronged you,' Ann answered.

He frowned. 'Oh to hell with it all,' he said. 'What's the point of this? Life is no civil court. What does it matter who is guilty of what? No one is going to award you or me any damages. There's no judge and no jury.'

'I wish there were a judge somewhere,' Ann said softly.

'I think you are a sweet lovely creature,' Philip said after a while, 'and I honestly feel I have nothing to forgive you for. That doesn't mean it's easy to get used to the idea of you and that damned painter kissing.'

'Oh Phil. Haven't you ever kissed anyone? Everybody kisses aunts and friends and mothers.'

'No,' he said angrily. 'I haven't and I couldn't, not since I've known you. And aunts and mothers are in a slightly different category – what fantastic nonsense.' While he answered her, he thought of Audrey Holding. But that was different, he told himself. It's the waiting which makes it different. I was waiting for Ann while she was fiddling around in that loft. And I'm a man. It's not the same.

She came over to him and put her hand on his forehead. 'Please dismiss the whole business from your mind. I don't care about any man in the world but you. Please try.'

'I'll try,' he said.

82

HE felt her waiting, expecting and not expecting a statement from him, a gesture which would set everything right.

He very much wanted to make it; he wanted it so much that it hurt. Sitting at his typewriter in the news agency, he would lose himself in thoughts of the many things he could do, a letter to her, a telegram, flowers. She is such a ceremony girl, he thought, she likes fresh-starts-and-new-dates games, she is such a gratifying person to make happy this way.

He phrased a telegram to her at the Foundation; and he pictured her reaction when she read it. He saw himself going there in the morning and having a bunch of roses sent up to her with a card saying, Happy Wednesday.

Then he said to himself, her first idea would probably be that the painter had sent it.

He was suddenly embittered against her by that thought. And he began to think about a dream he had had, a dream of which he only remembered that somehow, somewhere, 'he had been carried home.' 'I've come home,' he had said aloud, half-crying, waking himself up.

Where is that home? he asked himself. Ann must have been the home of that dream, otherwise it's all senseless; if she is not, I have lost my identity and I must go out into the world and search for it.

There were voices ringing in his ears, what is the matter with me, he thought, am I going mad? He stood up and went out into the silent corridor and walked to the wash-room; he closed the door and went over to the mirror. He stared at his face in the whitish trembling neon light. How odd I look, he said to himself, is this me? I am not that. What on earth has happened to me?

I knew who I was when I was very young, I knew who I was when I woke up as a boy, on a day in summer, before dawn, in the silent house.

I must go out and find my identity again.

Why does it seem as if I realized this today? Because of Ann and her painter? Am I not using that, using it as a lever against all our love, all our nostalgia, in order to be free? Or am I justified in feeling bitter against her, with the hope of fighting it and getting over it?

He did not know the answer; and he did not say anything to Ann.

83

IT was in those days that he was called one morning at the agency by Audrey Holding.

'How did you know I work here?' he asked, rather taken aback.

'You don't sound very pleased with my call,' she said.

'Oh I'm sorry, I didn't mean it that way. I was just surprised.'

'Someone told me, a journalist who knows you.'

'Oh,' Philip said.

'Have you been to California yet?' she asked.

'What? Oh no, that was postponed – until next month.'

He asked her about her job, and they talked a bit back and forth without Philip inviting her or suggesting anything. 'Oh heavens, Miss Holding,' he said aloud in a contemptuous voice when he had hung up.

During dinner he felt himself studying Ann in an oddly detached way. He said, 'I have a dinner tomorrow I have to go to, some press business. I hope you don't mind.'

Ann smiled at him. 'No, I don't mind. Who's giving the dinner?'

He frowned. 'Just some Organization.'

She raised her eyebrows.

'Damn it, Ann, I'm not a five-year-old,' he said quickly. 'Can't I go to a dinner and chew on dry chicken with a bunch of awful journalists without giving you full explanations first?'

'I was only showing some interest,' Ann said hurt. 'I don't give a damn about your journalists or your chicken. You can choke on it as far as I'm concerned.'

'Well, thank you very much. I guess that would suit you and your painter splendidly,' he said tonelessly.

'What did you say?' Ann asked.

'Nothing.'

The following morning he telephoned Audrey Holding. 'I'd like to invite you for dinner tonight,' he said in a low voice.

She was surprised. 'That's terribly sweet of you, Philip. I'd love to. But could you make it another evening, any other evening this week? Tonight I'm busy.'

He made a face at the telephone. 'No,' he said, unfriendly, 'I'm sorry, I can't any other night.'

There was a silence, then she said, 'Well, all right, then. I'll postpone my date for this evening. I'll come.'

He met Ann for lunch in a restaurant; she asked him, 'What time is your dinner?'

'At seven,' he answered. 'Downtown.'

'I guess you should go there straight from your office then.'

'Yes, that would be simplest,' he answered. He felt guilty and grateful because she had said that. He looked hard at her.

'When will you be home?' she asked.

'I've no idea. It might be late.'

'You should have put a white shirt on,' she said.

'Oh for heaven's sake, Ann, leave that to me,' he said.

Ann started cutting a piece of her meat and he stared fascinated at her hands; they're so well shaped, he thought, slender, pale, red nails.

'You know what, Philip,' she said without looking up from her plate and without interrupting her movement, 'I don't believe a word of that press dinner. I never did. And what's more interesting, I don't think I really care. Make it as late as you want to; as a matter of fact, perhaps it would be much simpler if you didn't come home at all.'

She reddened while saying that and he reddened too, but he did not answer.

84

THEY had stopped telephoning each other since the day after Ann's party with the painter; that day she had called and he had not answered her call. At five o'clock Philip looked at the telephone, but it did not ring. At half past five he found himself finished with his work. Tony expressed surprise that he didn't rush out as usual but returned to his desk. 'I have an hour to kill,' Philip explained.

'Come and have a drink with me,' Tony suggested.

Philip accepted half-heartedly; it was difficult to refuse.

During the afternoon he had told himself he would think things over when he was through working; now chance provided a way out. Somehow he could not really concentrate any more on what was at stake; he was drifting and could not stop it. I'm running away from something, he thought; but then again it seemed as if someone were pushing him. It's the Devil, he thought, that's what they'd have said two hundred years ago. And why not, it's me and the Devil in one person.

And in the meantime Tony chatted about the work and the people in the agency. Tony took the mechanics of life very seriously and, usually silent, now held forth at length about them; he didn't like his job but never questioned its role as a cog in the big machine, or the God-given nature of the machine. 'Don't be so eager, Tony,' Philip couldn't help saying at one point; he smiled and Tony smiled back, not knowing how to take this remark.

Then Philip took a subway to Fourteenth Street and walked to the Spanish restaurant where he was to meet Audrey Holding. He was late but he didn't hurry. That evening he liked the presence and the feeling of New York. Vague ideas flitted through his head, not quite translated into words; if the house in Ardsley had only worked. Then that led again to the painter kissing Ann's shoulder. He tried to stop his thoughts; he focused so hard on each street lamp as he walked past it that the light became blurred.

He was so distracted that he almost bumped into Audrey Holding who was waiting outside the restaurant.

'Hey,' she cried, 'where are you going?'

'Oh hello,' he said, 'I'm terribly sorry to have kept you waiting. That blasted subway –'

'That's all right,' she answered, 'but I'm starving. Let's go in.' She laughed at him.

He looked at her. So much had she become an abstract notion to toy with that it was a shock now to realize that she was a live woman, a lean girl with prominent bones and eager eyes.

85

PHILIP kept up a conversation with her during the long dinner; he studied her while talking but without much interest.
Her personality, her manners and mannerisms irritated him but
he was very aware of her presence as a woman.

Audrey Holding told him about a man who had been pur-
suing her for a long time now. He sounded quite attractive to
Philip and he asked, 'But what's so terrible about him?'

'His hands make me feel absolutely ill,' she said. And then
she added, 'You have wonderful hands. In fact I think you're
a most handsome man.'

Philip did not feel pleased with this. 'Doesn't it seem fantas-
tically unfair to you,' he asked, 'that people are judged by such
standards? Why should your life be determined by the length
of your fingers or the shape of your chin?'

'Oh, but character and appearance go together,' she said. 'If
I like somebody's face I also like his personality.'

'But that's only an acquired thing – ugly people aren't born
with different souls from handsome people; they become different because of the way society reacts to them. If you took a
very ugly little girl and completely isolated her somewhere,
with a nurse or parents who'd admire her, she would grow up
with the personality of a beautiful woman.'

'That's just what happened to me,' she said .

He began to laugh; that was the moment he liked her best.

86

SHE lived on Eighty-sixth Street at Park Avenue and he took her there after the dinner in a taxi; she talked and he looked at her and at the meter.

'I'll make us a drink,' she said, and he followed her up to her apartment on the second floor.

A light was burning in the hallway, which was papered in green; he put his raincoat down on a small varnished table. 'That's my room-mate's section,' she said, pointing at a door half-open to a dark room. 'It's a good layout, the bathroom is in between.' While she spoke she looked at herself in an old mirror over the table and smoothed her hair with her hand.

'Now I'll show you my place,' she said, and he followed her into a room at the other end of the hallway. She switched on a lamp; it had a shade with red birds and fishes on it.

'I only have gin,' she said, 'do you like gin and tonic?'

'Oh yes, sure.'

She made two drinks and sat on the couch with them. Philip was still standing; she handed him his glass and he sat down beside her. She took a sip and then pushed herself back until she leaned against the wall.

Reaching out, she put her glass on the floor; she looked at him. He leaned over and kissed her, holding his glass in his right hand; then he sat up straight again and said, 'I hope it doesn't all seem too obvious – I mean, first the dinner, and then this, it's so – '

'Don't be silly,' she said with a very warm smile and taking his glass away, put her arms around him.

It went all very fast; when he started to unzipp her dress, his heart beating wildly, she stood up and took it off herself. She undressed and lay back again. He kissed her on the mouth and then sat up and took off his own clothes. He touched her, and she was very excited; he came to her. She began to moan, and

143

when she had him she cried out his name several times, 'Oh Philip, Philip,' she sighed.

And he lay next to her and thought, How many names she must have called that way. It made him smile almost; she must have hesitated just one moment, he thought, just to make sure that she had got the right name. I can't make love to her again, I couldn't stand all that moaning and groaning. He kissed her lightly on her forehead and dressed.

It seemed to him that the first time he thought of Ann that evening was when he put his coat on in the hallway and saw himself in the stained glass of the mirror.

87

WHEN he came out into the street it was a quarter to twelve; how did it get so late, he wondered. He started walking east along Eighty-sixth Street.

It had been raining, a few drops were still falling; and the asphalt of the empty roadway reflected the lights of the movie house at the corner. As he reached it, they were turned off and the gleam of the street became dark. He bought a paper, and then he crossed the street and entered a cafeteria.

There were many people there, couples and lonely-looking men with newspapers and half-filled cups of coffee. He turned around and went back out into the street.

He stood at the corner, the light changed and he crossed with it. He walked up to a hot-dog stand and said, 'A frankfurter, please. No, an orange-juice.' The counter man filled the cup while talking in German to a neat-looking old man who sat on a crate of empty bottles.

And then Philip continued his walk. On a clock in a darkened shop window he saw that it was midnight. He unfolded his paper and looked at the headlines. The rain stopped altogether, and a light wind rose.

He was free.